Rise of Dragons – Book 1

Awakening

G Clatworthy

Find more at www.gemmaclatworthy.com

Cover art by Sanjay Charlon (Beehive Illustrations)

Foreword

Thank you to the amazing first readers, terrific typo hunters and grammar gurus – you are awesome!

Come and join my readers' Facebook group, Gemma's Book Wyrms, for updates and chat about dragons or find me on www.instagram.com/gemmaclatworthy and join my mailing list at www.gemmaclatworthy.com or my patreons at www.patreon.com/G_Clatworthy

Chapter 1

I tugged my hand through my thick brown hair, wondering if I needed to wash it before meeting Aloora, my gnomish friend, for drinks later. I was thinking about closing early to get in a quick shower. My hand snagged on my enchanted welding goggles I was wearing on my head. They weren't standard goggles and I'd had them made in the steampunk style I favoured; brown leather and brass studs. I'd even paid extra for brown rather than black tinted lenses. They helped me see the enchantments I worked on my own magical jewellery and were part of my everyday wear in the shop.

I sensed a magical presence outside the shop but thought nothing of it. Many magical and half magical beings live in Cardiff, tolerated by the mundane beings albeit mostly ignored. It wasn't unusual for them to pass through Royal Arcade to visit any of the boutique shops housed there. Gundersson's Dwarven Delicatessen, in particular, was a perennial favourite and was a couple of doors down from my own jewellery shop.

The silver bell outside my shop tinkled merrily and the door opened. I stifled a sigh. So much for closing early and having a wash.

An elf entered, tall and slender with long blonde hair hanging loose to his shoulders. He was dressed in ripped jeans and a dark green shirt, tucked in at the front but casually untucked at the back. I was immediately on guard. Elves were notorious snobs and I'd had problems in the past when elven customers sensed I was only a half-dwarf and not full blooded. They hadn't been overly aggressive. Being elves, they were more about snide comments than outright fighting. The comments hurt though and dented my confidence, which was always fragile when comparing my short, stocky frame to willowy golden elves.

I caught his eye with a shopkeeper's smile on my face. It wasn't as if I could afford to turn away any business if I wanted to save enough to buy my own place. I stopped my thoughts from wandering to luxurious, tastefully decorated Victorian detached houses that I frequently looked up on property websites, even though they were outrageously above my price range, and launched into my welcoming spiel.

"Welcome to Amethyst's Treasures, providing jewellery and artefacts for any occasion," I mirrored the chirpy sign outside, "I'm Amethyst, how may I be of service?"

He looked me up and down, with a haughty gaze as if he'd summed me up in one look. His eyes paused on my goggles, shoved into my bushy brown hair before moving down to meet my eyes. He gracefully walked across the wooden floors where I stood behind the painted white counter. Flecks of darker wood shone through the white paint, giving it a distressed look I called "shabby chic" but Aloora called "just shabby".

"How indeed?" he murmured in a deep voice with a Welsh accent. He was attractive as all elves were, and this close his glamour was palpable. He almost seemed to glow with a golden aura. I found myself blushing as his green eyes dropped to my chest and then back again. I could see why people fainted over elves and thought briefly of the pop singer Cirian who had been in the press recently when record numbers of fans had fainted at his latest concert at the Millennium Stadium here in Cardiff.

Annoyed with myself for being taken in by his glamour, I echoed his gaze, dropping my eyes to his trousers and back to his eyes whilst reaching for my ancestral axe, Bane. It was named for the famous axe held by dragon slayer Lieffson. I placed it calmly on the counter between us. My father, renowned weapons forger, Dafydd Haernson, had given me the blue steel axe as a coming of age present and it was infused with runes and dwarfish magic. I wasn't usually so aggressive with customers but the act of touching it immediately countered any elvish glamour and I left my hand on it as I replied.

"You are looking for some jewellery perhaps?"

The sight of the axe made him back up and he moved away to peruse the glass display cases in my shop. I considered leaving him to it, but in truth I needed a sale so, leaving the axe on the counter, I walked lightly to his side.

"Those charms offer protection," I offered, noticing his eyes on the steel beads that made up my charm range, "and they go well with these braids." I indicated the woven leather braids on the shelf below, wondering if he was buying for himself or someone else.

He moved his hand to the case and tried to open it. I smiled as he couldn't manipulate the dwarfish lock charms I had placed over the very secure human padlocks I had purchased.

I let him struggle for a moment more before stepping in. "Allow me," I held up my key. It looked ordinary, at least to human eyes, but it contained the magic required to open these and indeed most locks.

I took the tray holding the protection charms out of the case and held it out for him to have a closer look. Unfortunately, this meant it was in front of my chest or more accurately my large boobs, currently pressed upwards in a leather corset with steampunk-like brass clasps. I willed myself not to blush and inwardly cursed my love of steampunk fashion, and that I was already dressed to go out with Aloora tonight.

He had the grace to look moderately uncomfortable and even gave a nervous cough.

"Yes, I need protection. Which is the strongest charm?" he asked with a note of strain in his voice.

I selected my most powerful charm in the case and handed it to him, noticing the callouses on his palm as he held his hand out. An archer, I wondered. I wasn't surprised, many elves practised archery. They had even pulled some strings to hold weekly practice sessions in the grounds of Cardiff Castle, a favour I couldn't imagine being granted to other magical races. He nodded as it touched his palm, sensing the magic.

"It has innate magic," I told him, "it will compel most who intend to harm you to turn away."

"Most?" he queried with an eyebrow raised.

"Powerful magic users may not be affected, I cannot guarantee 100% effectiveness," aware I wasn't doing a great sales job, I smoothed my voice and added, "it does also have an activation word. Say the Dwarfish word "sheld" and an invisible barrier will appear, stopping any but the most powerful magic users from getting close, for around 10 minutes."

"10 minutes…I see. Yes, I'll take it," He closed his hand around the charm and walked towards the counter whilst I re-secured the remaining charms in the display cabinet.

I stepped back behind the counter and priced it up, stopping myself from asking if he'd like it gift wrapped when I noticed he'd already strung it onto a plaited leather band on his wrist. He hesitated as he handed over the money, resting his palm on mine. It felt soft and cool against my warm and calloused hands. No matter how much expensive hand cream I used, my hands were toughened by years assisting my father and working at my own smaller forge. I could feel something else as well; a sensation similar to the buzz of electricity. Elvish magic I assumed, though I wasn't an expert.

The axe was still on top of the counter and I considered grabbing it when he started to speak softly, not quite meeting my gaze.

"I, uh, hear you are also a, uh, weapon smith…" he let the words hang, flicking his green eyes to meet mine before lowering them to the floor.

So that was it. He wanted quality dwarven craftsman – or woman-ship either without paying dwarven prices or without the weapons being registered.

Any weapons made by full-blooded dwarves were added to the Dwarven Arms Council register and were technically not for sale but were rather leased, although those leases could last for thousands of years. However, should any dwarf-forged weapons be found attacking dwarves, that lease could be instantly revoked and the owners would find themselves suddenly at the attention of some heavily armed bureaucrats from the Dwarven Arms Council requesting the weapons back with extreme prejudice.

It was true, I had made magical weapons before, and I was glad my reputation for quality workwomanship was getting out, so I hesitated only briefly before nodding.

"What are you after? I have some limited stock here or if you wanted something more bespoke…"

I didn't finish the sentence but the time and cost of a bespoke item was implied.

"I will look at your stock," he responded, "I need something today."

"Oh?" I asked.

"I was told your silence is part of the service," the elf glowered at me.

"It is," I replied, "but I would like to know if I'm going to get questioned about any activity my weapons might be involved in…my silence then costs extra."

"I can pay," he replied

"Right," I breathed, elongating the vowel and making it clear I didn't quite believe him. Still, I would now add a hundred to my price. "Follow me," I said, turning and walking into the back room that held my small forge. Unlike the shop, the floor here was slate and my brick forge was built into the existing chimney. The previous owner had been complaining of draughts and strange noises from the chimney so not only was I paying a bargain rent, I had been able to put in my own forge after clearing the birds' nests from the chimney.

Errol, my wyrm, a small creature said to be a descendent of dragons, lifted his red head. He had been a coming of age present from my Uncle Owain, a wyrm breeder with no eyebrows and a perpetually singed beard. Errol opened his amber eyes and tilted his head as if to ask if he would be working tonight.

"I might need you later," I confirmed in a soft voice, reaching out to scratch his head. I was never quite sure if Errol understood me but he reached his head into a bucket of coal next to him and ate a lump. He would be fuelled if I did need his fire tonight.

I turned back to the elf, who was looking at my wyrm with something approaching amazement in his eyes.

“That’s Errol,” I said nonchalantly. I wondered if he had ever seen a wyrm before. They were eclectic pets but not endangered and I sometimes saw them on the streets on stout chain-link leads. They were status symbols for the elite, especially the golden coloured ones and I had even once seen one perched like a Chihuahua in a pink Prada handbag. Judging by the smoke rising from the wyrm’s nostrils, I hadn’t fancied the handbag’s chances and a shriek a little later on had confirmed it. The wyrm had escaped into Bute Park and I had laughed heartily as I had regaled the tale to Uncle Owain later that night.

“Errol?” the elf asked with one perfect eyebrow arched.

“Errol,” I repeated, “Like the dragon in the Discworld novels…you know, by Terry Pratchett,” I added as he still looked confused. He immediately went down even further in my estimation as it was clear he had never read any Discworld books.

“Right,” he replied, clearly trying to fake it.

I stifled a disapproving noise that had automatically tried to leave my throat and managed to turn it into a passably convincing cough. I reached under my metal workbench and pulled out a black roll of cloth. As I unfurled it, I was satisfied to hear a gasp from the elf. He clearly wasn’t expecting the beauty or deadliness of the blades I had unveiled.

There were several small daggers, being faster to make and easier to store but I also had one pair of throwing axes and two longer swords in my collection.

The elf contemplated the swords, picking them up and testing them as best as he could in the small room. He eventually settled on the longer one. I wondered if it was because of the green leather I’d wrapped carefully around the hilt. He lifted his finger to touch the blade.

"Don't," I stopped him. He looked confused so I continued, "It's very sharp and ready to be enchanted. It wants blood and will cut you no matter how careful you are. These aren't for show."

"Good," he replied and he looked carefully at the blade before putting it back down. "Can you add any other enchantments?"

I squinted and rubbed the back of my neck. Of course I could, but I would charge him a pretty penny for the privilege. "What did you have in mind?" I asked, pitching my voice in what I hoped was a tone that wouldn't convey I was already back to dreaming of Victorian detached houses…with gardens.

"My friend has been…taken," he stated as a response. "I'm going to get her back and need any help I can get. Protection, luck, accuracy…what can you do?"

I hadn't expected to get any information out of him, so I was taken aback but quickly recovered. I bit back my immediate question about whether the police were involved. The mundane police force wasn't quick to pursue magical kidnappings and the Magical Liaison Office weren't that much better.

"I can enchant the sword with many runes, but it won't be cheap."

He nodded as if he was expecting that.

"And it will take time, I can have it for you next week."

"I need it tonight," now he sounded exasperated, "How much can you do tonight?"

"I'm going out, to meet *my* friend," I replied.

He threw a bag onto my workbench. It jangled heavily. Curious, I opened it. It was more money than I would usually make in a month. Playing it cool, I placed the money in a drawer next to my workbench and looked him in the eye.

"That will pay for my time today. This sword can adequately hold four enchantments, any more and it may start to split apart with power."

"I thought dwarfish blades were strong," he put an edge to his voice but we both knew he wouldn't back out of our deal now.

I put an equal edge to my voice, "As I said, bespoke costs extra. I didn't fashion these blades to take more than four enchantments. That is more than adequate," I paused then added, "…for a competent swordsman."

His eyes narrowed at that, "I am a competent swordsman."

"Then four enchantments should be sufficient," I replied smoothly, "now, what would you like? I would recommend protection, true strike, luck and heat or ice, but you know more about how you're going to use it."

"I'll need all the luck I can get," he almost cracked a smile, almost, "so yes luck, true strike, protection and…" he paused considering another option, "ice," he decided finally.

I nodded, took my phone out to text Aloora I would be late, locked the shop, pulled my goggles over my eyes and then got to work.

The elf had taken the seat in my shop as I worked the blade in the back room with the door pushed shut. I wouldn't let anyone see me working on this crucial part of the enchanting process, I may only be a half-dwarf but I protected their secrets as my dad had taught me.

It took two hours of work with Errol lending me his heat, but I was satisfied with the result. The runes were etched beautifully in the hilt and I had no doubt they would work perfectly. I called him through and presented the sword.

"This rune represents luck, it will automatically make you lucky with hits and blocks when you are wielding the sword. There will also be some residual luck when you are carrying the sword on your person without drawing it. You might get lucky on a scratch card but I wouldn't bet on a full lottery win."

I pointed to the second rune. This one seemed to glow blue in the light of my forge.

"This one is true strike; again it doesn't need a word to activate it and the sword will be more likely to hit your intended target, although if you're wildly off with your aim, it won't help." I couldn't resist the jibe at his swordsmanship. His eyes narrowed but he let me continue.

"It will also make your sword seem thirsty for blood," I rushed on as he seemed about to interrupt, "I can't explain it well, but you'll know in battle. It's like when in the songs the famous blades are battle hungry, you might sense something like that from this blade, although it won't be as strong as Bloodbane."

The elf nodded. Everyone had heard of Lieffson and his trusty axe, Bloodbane. It had been one of my favourite tales growing up and my dwarven kin often sang it on the alleged anniversary of the slaying of Meltar, the fire breathing dragon who had terrorised earth millennia ago. Supposedly my family were related to the famous dwarf. I didn't believe it, mainly because practically every dwarven clan claimed a relation to several of the old dwarves of legend. Either they were particularly promiscuous or, more likely, the clans made parts of their heritage up, similar to British kings and queens, when creating family trees. Still, our family's ancestral axe was called Bane in honour of our proclaimed relation to Lieffson. I was surprised the Dwarven Arms Council allowed it. They were usually hot on protecting the names of famous weapons, but one of my real ancestors had led the Council at one point so he'd probably pushed through any paperwork needed.

"And this is protection, the same as the charm you purchased earlier. It works the same and the same word "sheld" will put up the same barrier. As you have two of the same enchantments, the barrier will be doubly hard to penetrate but will last the same amount of time."

The final rune glowed white and as I touched it. It seemed cold even in the heat of the forge.

"This is ice. Say "rhew" and the blade will become like frost. Good for breaking through heat resistance or cooling your drinks," as I said the word, the blade did indeed seem to acquire a coating of ice.

Against my previous advice, the elf touched the blade then immediately withdrew his hand, shaking it in pain.

"Good work," he commented. I was amazed at the compliment and satisfied myself with a grunt of acknowledgment as I sheathed the sword in a leather scabbard the same shade of green as the wrappings on the hilt.

I held it out in two hands to him, a traditional dwarfish gesture acknowledging the gifting of a powerful weapon with respect to an equal. He solemnly held out his two hands palm up to receive the sword, either knowing the custom or feeling like it was somehow the right thing to do.

After receiving the sword, he looked at the belt loop on the scabbard and the thick belt he was wearing with his jeans. He looked confounded for a second before placing the sword back down on my workbench and starting to unfasten his belt buckle.

My eyebrows shot up before I could stop them and he transitioned from slightly embarrassed and awkward to arrogant in a moment, giving me a salacious grin as he removed his belt. Then he turned his attention to threading the sword onto the thick leather.

"It's illegal to carry magical weapons without a permit you know," I stated the obvious. It wasn't illegal to make or sell the weapons but their owners had to have a permit. I should have checked before making the sale, or at least before he'd strung it onto his belt. Damned if I was going anywhere near his trousers to try to remove it.

"I have a permit," he replied haughtily, not offering to show it to me, "besides, I have magic," he spoke a word in Elvish and started walking out of the forge and across the shop. As he approached the door, the sword disappeared from my sight.

Invisibility…maybe I should start adding that enchantment as standard, I thought, before the business dwarf in me added, or as an extra cost.

He left the shop, still doing up the buckle, and spoke suggestively over his shoulder.

"Thank you for your… services, Amethyst half-dwarf."

Elvish cul I cursed in Dwarfish, the best language for cursing or swearing of any kind, as I glimpsed the last remaining customers walking through the Arcade. They had obviously heard his comment and were looking with curious eyes in my direction. I firmly shut and locked the door. I was definitely done for tonight.

After he'd left, and I'd calmed down, I pulled off my goggles. I wound my hair into two sturdy plaits and twined them together, the only style my thick half dwarven hair was able to handle without copious amounts of hair product. A quick glance in the mirror that my customers used showed I was presentable even if I did still have a silhouette of the goggles etched around my eyes.

I strode into the forge and petted Errol on his head, scratching behind his small wing shaped ears.

"Good job tonight boy," I assured him and he leaned into the scratch. "I'm going out now to see Aloora, see you later," He gave a contented grunt and settled down. I had thought a wyrm would be a good guard for my shop, given their reputation for being snappish and setting fire to things but Errol was always loving and affectionate, rarely growling and only blowing flames when I needed his help with my forging.

I gave him one last tickle behind the ear and strode back through my shop to grab the red woollen coat that I had hung on the back of my chair behind the counter. I rarely needed it as I ran hot, thanks to my dwarfish blood but there had been a chill in the spring air recently.

I enjoyed putting my coat on as always. The lining slipped across my back and shoulders and the lamb's wool was soft against my hands and cheek as I flattened the lapels down. I did up the sturdy, black fabric buttons, and as I looked again in the mirror on the shop floor, I knew that it flattered my curves and had been worth the money I'd spent on it on an impulse to shut my mother up during a long shopping trip across Cardiff. After all, a good coat was an investment, as mother would say, and it was. I looked presentable and buying it had satisfied my mother enough to stop her nagging me about getting something respectable to wear…that day anyway.

I walked out of the door and stepped into the coolness of an empty Royal Arcade. I took a breath and pulled the metal shutters down on my shop, locking it both with the mundane heavy-duty padlocks and the magical locks learned from my father. Once I was sure that everything was secured, I marched to the pub where I had arranged to meet Aloora, my heavy-soled leather boots causing my footsteps to echo on the tiled floor of the Arcade.

Chapter 2

I walked briskly to the Rummer Tavern, one of our favourite pubs. It wasn't far but the March air had a cool, spring chill to it, reminding those of us foolish enough to be outside that winter was still close and hadn't yet left Wales.

I stuffed my hands into the pockets of my expensive red coat and hunched my shoulders against the wind, glad at least that it wasn't raining, as I skilfully wound my way through the puddles that lay on the ground from a previous spring shower.

I was glad of the bright streetlights that illuminated the way as the spring nights fell early here, although my dad had passed on his night vision to me. Dwarves were very good at seeing in the dark, having spent millennia living underground. Nowadays only the strict dwarves lived in mines and all the ones I knew had adapted well to living in houses, although they were always keen to avoid thatched cottages for fear of perpetuating stereotypes from cartoons.

Soon I was at the Rummer and the warm, yellow lights spilled onto the grey pavement, welcoming me in and promising relief from the chill night air.

I walked in and was instantly too warm in my thick coat and leather corset style top. I scanned the room, looking for Aloora. I didn't see my gnomish friend but I did spot an empty table. These were at a premium in the cosy pub so I marched over to it and sat down quickly on a wobbly stool before the regulars standing at the bar spotted it.

I took my coat off, earning a couple of hungry looks from some of the other customers. I groaned inwardly. I was in no mood to be hit on and regretted my choice of top, which showed off my ample breasts. Normally Aloora and I would have laughed and maybe even welcomed the attention but tonight all I wanted was a couple of drinks and maybe something to eat with my friend, when she arrived.

I stuffed my coat onto the spare seat at the small wooden table to dissuade any attention and rang Aloora. No answer. I thought about leaving a message but she didn't listen to them so I texted her instead.

Hey Ally, I've got a table at the back of Rummer. See you soon x

I looked up and considered the bar. If I left the table it might be taken, but I was thirsty and, after my encounter with the elf, in need of alcohol. I cursed inwardly, wishing I had more items of clothing to leave on the chair and waited a couple of minutes for an opening at the bar then stood. I spread my coat as best I could over both stools and the table, grateful it was knee-length and had a lot of fabric before shouldering my way to the bar.

I caught the half-troll bartender's attention immediately with my cleavage and he walked over.

"What can I get you?" he drooled, addressing my chest.

"Two cokes, one with vodka, a lime and soda and a bowl of chips," I ordered, handing him a note and nodding towards the small table I had nabbed. I thought about adding a chocolate fudge cake to the order as The Rummer had one of the best in the city, but Aloora might want to eat too and I could always order it later.

“Shouldn’t dwarves drink beer?” he asked with what he probably thought was a charming smile and dazzling wit, but I was in no mood for banter.

“Half-dwarves drink what they want,” I informed him, clearly not interested. His smile dropped and he went back to pouring the drinks. He smiled again as he handed me the drinks and my change, and informed me that my chips would be out soon, but it was clear his heart wasn’t in it after my cool reception and he was already looking at two troll ladies who had just entered the bar before he finished speaking.

I liked the openness of the Rummer to all comers, magical and mundane. It reminded me of home, brought up by my dwarfish Dad and human Mum. I straddled both worlds and frequently felt like I didn’t truly fit in either.

I was more careful as I edged my way back to the table to avoid spilling drinks and I made it without spilling a drop until I tried to place them onto the table. It seemed to have all four legs at different heights and I spilled a good amount of my cola on the table and my coat.

“Schiztz,” I breathed, switching easily to Dwarfish for swearing. I finished putting the drinks down and picked up my coat. I dabbed at it half-heartedly with some paper napkins on the table but it made little difference other than causing tiny bits of tissue paper to stick to the wet stain on my coat.

I put it behind me at an angle so I wouldn’t get wet and glared at the cola as if that had caused all this trouble. I downed the brown drink, enjoying the sweet taste and the bubbles going down my throat, slaking my thirst. I imagined Aloora's comments.

That stuff will rot your teeth.

Hardly. My ancestors had grown up eating dwarven battle bread, so a fizzy brown drink wasn't going to damage their teeth.

Your human ancestors didn't.

Imaginary Aloora was committed to her cause, namely making me eat and drink more healthily. I didn't have a response to that so I slurped down the final bit of cola and switched to my vodka and coke.

I sipped the alcoholic drink slowly, enjoying the slightly tarter taste compared to the sweet cola I'd just downed. I closed my eyes and sighed, acknowledging that I was finally relaxing after the encounter with the elf cul.

I called Aloora again. Still no answer. I wondered if she was at the library still, nose deep in ancient texts as she studied some dragon lore or ancient language or if she was hurrying here right now, dodging the raindrops that had started to fall. I texted again.

Are you on your way? I'm right at the back. See you soon x

I left the phone on the table and eyed it to make sure it had signal and the text had gone through.

I had slowly sipped my way through half my drink when the golden chips arrived. The smell of them made my mouth water and I picked one up and munched it, enjoying the crunch as I slathered the rest of the chips with salt, vinegar and mountains of tomato sauce.

I ate them too quickly as usual, favouring the crunchy ones and finishing with the fluffier chips. I ended up swirling the remaining chip in the dregs of the salt and vinegar and ketchup at the bottom of the bowl before licking my fingers to get the last bit of flavour from the dish. I couldn't help it, I loved fried food.

My head lifted every time the door opened, letting in a blast of the chill wind and showering those standing close to the entrance with rain. Aloora still wasn't here. The latest she'd ever been was two hours, and she'd turned up then with pink cheeks gushing about a new Elvish text the librarian had managed to get on loan from the British Library which she had just had to start translating right away.

That had been an exception though and there was an uneasy feeling in the pit of my stomach that the food had done nothing to quell. I picked up my phone from the table and checked my social media accounts.

Aloora was a minor celebrity in the city thanks to her obsession with dragons and all things ancient and frequently posted videos of herself reading texts or pictures of her latest book acquisitions. There had been no posts since six p.m., right when I was dealing with the elf so I assumed she'd got my message that I'd be late.

I glanced at the digital display in the top right hand corner. Nine p.m. That was three hours ago. Very unusual. The knot in my stomach tightened. She usually posted almost hourly, even when we were out together, which was annoying but she was a good friend and it helped my business too, so I put up with it. I sent direct messages to all her accounts and texted her again.

Ally, are you OK? X

I made myself wait another ten minutes and glugged my drink down impatiently. Still no reply. I sent one final text, hoping she'd call.

Ally, where are you? I'm going to the library. CALL ME x

I grabbed my coat and stood up. A couple who had been eyeing the table for some time sank into the wooden stools gratefully, frowning slightly at the chips and glasses I'd left. I elbowed my way to the door, the press of bodies starting to feel suffocating, especially as I could sense magical auras from several of them. The combination of magic and anxiety for Aloora was starting to give me a headache and I forced myself to breathe slowly as I entered the chill night air.

A couple of humans were huddling under the eaves by the doorway smoking home rolled cigarettes. I breathed in the smoke as well as the air and stifled a cough. Glaring at them, I stepped into the rain and pulled on my coat, doing it up tightly as I walked briskly towards the university's central library.

Once my coat was fastened I moved in a sort of half run, half fast walk in an effort to get to the library quickly whilst ensuring I didn't need to stop to grab my breath. The rain glinted orange in the glow of the streetlights and I was glad of my thick leather boots as I moved through the large puddles that formed on the uneven pavements.

I decided not to cut through the park in front of the museum and instead stuck to the well-lit roads, dodging cars as well as puddles rather than walking to the crossing points. It was stupid and two cars beeped their horns loudly in displeasure as I ran in front of them. I gave them a thank you wave and continued speedily towards the library.

As I arrived, I slowed my pace. I would need to talk to the security guard and librarian and I didn't want to be out of breath. I got a weird feeling on my neck like I was being watched and I turned up the collar on my thick coat, as if that would offer some protection, against what, I didn't know.

Then I noticed big amber eyes watching me from under one of the dirty cars parked outside the off-white student building that housed the library.

A wyrm. It slunk closer as I walked past and I noticed steam coming from its blunt snout. A stray wyrm by the look of it, no relation of a dragon would choose to be out in this downpour if it had a home. I considered calling to it, but I didn't want to lure it out of its hiding spot and it might not like the smell of Errol on me. I thought briefly about trying to capture it for my Uncle but I didn't have anything to handle it with and stray wyrms could be dangerous. I decided I would tell Uncle Owain about it, maybe he could come and get it or call whichever rescue charity dealt with wyrms.

I walked into the building and was immediately stopped by a call from the security guard on duty tonight. He had clearly expected a quiet night and looked up from his tabloid newspaper with an amused look on his face.

"Did you swim here?" he asked, then laughed at his own joke.

I forced myself to smile back. I was soaking. I ran my fingers over my sodden hair. Normally bushy, it was now plastered to my head and water was running in rivulets down my face and shoulders. I started to unbutton my coat, it was warm in here and I was hot after my exertion to get here quickly.

"Something like that," I replied, "It's raining cats and dogs out there," I added as if it wasn't obvious.

I walked towards the plastic window and wooden counter that he sat behind, knowing I'd have to sign in to access the library.

"What are you doing here then?"

"I'm looking for my friend; she hangs out in the library a lot. Maybe you've seen her?" I added hopefully. "She's a bit shorter than me, thin, short black spiky hair, probably wearing a black coat with a dragon on it and a brown satchel. Maybe carrying a pile of books or some scrolls?"

"Aye, I know who you're talking about. She was here earlier for sure."

"And now….?" I prompted, trying not to lose patience.

"I'll check the sign in sheet."

As I waited, I looked around and appreciated my surroundings, as I always did. I loved the history of the place, shown in the paintings on the wall, the faded rich red carpet, and the bronze details on door handles. It was slightly marred by the university's standard font signs in English and Welsh pointing out directions to lecture halls, study rooms and the library.

"Looks like she signed out about seven o clock," the security guard's voice pulled my attention back to the window. He was pointing to an entry in the book. Underneath his ragged fingernail, I could indeed see Aloora's neat cursive handwriting signing herself out.

"Damn," I muttered under my breath, "thanks for that," I said more loudly, smiling again at the guard as I refastened my coat.

I turned and walked back to the large wooden doors and paused with my hand on the bulky round brass handle, deciding what to do next. Perhaps she went home after the library, if she had books with her, she wouldn't want to lug them to the pub.

"Pull it love," the security guard said helpfully.

I decided not to reply and instead yanked the door open all the way so he would get a blast of cold air as I left.

Chapter 3

As I walked quickly across the car park, I again felt like I was being watched. I looked directly under the car this time and as I expected, the wyrm was still there, amber eyes watching me as I walked past. I blinked. There was more than one pair of eyes under the car.

I felt more eyes on my back and turned. There was a black wyrm winding its way from the other side of the car park and across the stone steps by the entrance, blocking my way back in. I wanted to leave anyway so I started back towards the large iron gates, which were always open, heading towards the road.

The two wyrms left their spot under the dirt spattered Nissan and started towards me. Now they were in the light, I could see the colour of their scales. One appeared orange, although that might have been a trick of the orange street lamps. The other was a dark red, almost black. They were both the size of large cats but I had never worried about a gang of street cats before.

They moved slowly but deliberately like the predators they were. Their bodies steamed as the rain pelted them. At the same time, another black wyrm circled around from the other side of the car park. It had one large amber eye and a large scar down the left side of its face, across its other eye. It was making its way towards the gate, its body low to the ground and its one eye on me. This one was the size of a large dog. I guessed it was their leader judging by its tail curling with its point upwards. Alphas always pointed their triangular tails upwards rather than down.

I had read in the local paper about packs of wild wyrms roaming in Bute Park amidst calls to put the creatures on a registered animals list, but I'd never seen more than two together. I had never seen this many in one place outside of Uncle Owain's compound. They were clearly working as a pack and circling me. I wasn't sure half-dwarves were their usual dinner but if their fire was as hot as Errol's, I was screwed.

I felt in my pockets and was disappointed but unsurprised to find that I only had my phone in its red and yellow case with my cards stuffed in the inside and my keys. I promised myself that if I survived, I would take my axe with me everywhere.

I took the phone out and tried to decide who to call as I inched towards the gate. I walked slightly to the left as the leader wound to the right. As I tried to activate the emergency call function with shaking hands and whilst keeping my eyes on the leader, I accidently turned on my torch.

Not what I had intended to do, but I shined it directly into the alpha's eye. It winced and lowered its black head. That was all the distraction I was going to get and I took it. I started to run. I was past the alpha and out of the tall iron gates. I ran along the university's drive towards the road and was halfway there before they caught up with me.

One snapped at my calf. I was glad for the thick leather boots I was wearing. I spun faster than it was expecting and stamped on it hard. I brought my foot down again on the red head that was trying to bite through my boot. I heard something crunch and it let go, shaking its head and whimpering.

As I was stamping, one of the black wyrms had grabbed my coat with its powerful jaws. I felt it tug as it tried to pull me to the ground. I tried to resist, whilst turning so I could keep an eye on the other two wyrms that were circling me. The beast was strong despite its smaller size and I wasn't able to pull away. I leaned towards it suddenly and it was taken off balance. I used the moment of confusion to jab my thumbs into its eyes, a weak spot I was glad I knew about. It cried in pain and let go of my coat, taking a piece of red wool with it.

Two down. I hoped.

As soon as the black wyrm had released me, the remaining two pounced at once. I was knocked to the ground and swore as the tarmac grazed my side. Luckily I hadn't been winded and rolled with the fall. I managed to get my arms up as the smaller orange one tried to snap at my face. It connected with my forearm and I cried out as its teeth sank in.

I pulled my knee up and heaved myself onto my front, taking my assailant with me. I let all my weight fall onto the orange wyrm and it let go, more concerned with being squashed than biting my arm. I manoeuvred my free arm onto its neck and leaned into it. It started scrabbling at its throat with its forelegs and trying to claw me with its back legs, but my weight prevented it from getting purchase.

As I leaned in further, I felt something grab my foot hard. I turned my head to look over my shoulder and saw the large black wyrm had clamped onto my leather boot. I turned over, not releasing the orange one and aimed a kick at its head. It connected hard.

The wyrm backed off but was now thoroughly pissed at me and I saw its nostrils smoke as it prepared to breathe fire.

“Schiztz!” I cried and launched myself upwards, pushing the orange wyrm underneath me into the hard tarmac. I felt rather than heard something break. I focused on running away rather than feeling guilty as I fled towards the road. The wyrm followed me, waiting until I was within range of its flames rather than wasting an attack.

I made it across the road before my lungs and legs gave up. I had to stop outside the concrete pillars that marked the stairway that led to the Students Union. I turned and forced myself to take deep breaths as I faced the alpha. It had slowed down and was calmly walking towards me across the lanes that were empty of traffic on this spring night.

It stopped in the middle of the nearest lane to me and opened its mouth wide. I closed my eyes and raised my arms to protect my face when I heard an awful noise. Somewhere between a bang, a crunch of bone and a shriek of pain.

I opened my eyes and saw a city bus had rolled to a stop just past where I was standing. I walked over to it and spotted the wyrm under its second lot of wheels. It was crushed and no longer a danger to anyone.

The blue bus had a dent in the front and one of its tyres had burst as it had run over the creature. It wasn’t going anywhere tonight.

The passengers were starting to get out of the brightly lit bus and lined up on the pavement, sheltering under the large concrete stairwell of the Union. Several of them looked at me with fear and I realised I must look awful. My coat was wet and torn, my arm was bleeding. My hair was halfway out of its braids and my pinstriped leggings were ripped where I’d hit the tarmac.

The adrenaline was starting to leave me and I began to shake. I probably looked like I did drugs and I didn’t blame the bus passengers for judging me and wanting to keep their distance.

I sank down to the ground and leant against one of the uncomfortable concrete pillars, not caring that my boots were in the rain. I was already soaked and more rain couldn't hurt.

The driver was muttering about stray dogs and rubbing his head as he surveyed the damage to the front of his bus. He started to call for a replacement and I thought about staying to catch the bus to Aloora's house.

A concerned lady with permed blonde hair looked at me and walked over.

"Are you alright dear?" she asked, radiating concern.

I thought about telling the truth. I wasn't alright. A pack of stray wyrms had just attacked me and my best friend was either missing or ignoring me. Tonight sucked and I had a feeling it was going to be a long one. Instead I sighed heavily and forced myself to my feet.

"Fine thanks, just trying to find my friend," I replied in a flat voice. I had to focus on walking and couldn't give any energy to making my voice sound convincing.

"Well…if you're sure dear," The lady replied, looking at me as if she didn't believe a word of it. I definitely didn't believe it but I had to find Aloora.

I turned and walked, slowly this time, towards her ground floor student flat in a Victorian terrace off Miskin Street. This had once been a relatively smart street with neat terraced houses clad in brownish grey stone-effect brick and with large bay windows jutting into the small front gardens. Now the gardens had been paved with concrete slabs and were student housing, meaning they weren't well looked after.

Weeds sprung from between the paving. The houses looked eerie in the murky, orange half-light of the electric streetlights, with strange shadows forming at the entrances as porches hid the doors from view. Lights shone softly from behind cheap curtains and music was blaring from one of the houses. A metal tune I didn't recognise. The shabby front gardens of student housing and the multitude of black bin bags piled on the pavement added to the uneasy atmosphere.

A small tabby cat crossed the road in front of me as I turned into the street. I watched it carefully. I made sure I stayed in the street light and had the emergency services number tapped into my phone ready to call in case I was attacked a second time.

My left arm throbbed and was still bleeding, slow drops dripping onto the hundred-year old patterned tiles in the porch of Aloora's house as I lifted my good arm to knock on the door with my knuckles whilst I held my smartphone.

I paused. The door was ajar. That was unusual. I gripped my phone more tightly, my thumb over the dial symbol and I pushed the door open.

Chapter 4

I groped along the wall. The wallpaper was rough against my skin, being the hard wearing raised type that was often used in student accommodation and I felt my way towards the hallway light switch.

I found it and turned it on. The light worked and the bare lightbulb shone brightly showing me that the hall was empty and I had smeared blood on the wallpaper as I'd edged towards the light switch.

I grimaced, not so much from the pain which had now become a dull constant in my arm and down my side where I had hit the tarmac, but I might have cost my friend her deposit.

Aloora's room was on the ground floor and I walked the few paces towards the plain wooden door with a ceramic plaque attached declaring "Gnome at work". It was also open. I had a bad feeling as I approached. There was a large dent and a crack in the wood as if it had been kicked or something, or someone, I added mentally, had been thrown against it.

I pushed the door open warily but whoever had been there was long gone. I walked in and flipped the switch. The light illuminated a ransacked room. Aloora wasn't naturally neat, but she took care of her books and the scrolls and manuscripts she owned or borrowed to study. Her normal organisation system was organised chaos with stacks of papers on her desk and on the two deep bookshelves either side of the bricked-up fireplace with a coal-effect electric fire fastened to it.

Now the floor was covered with books and papers as if someone had been looking for something. The drawers of her desk were open, revealing more papers and stationery supplies crammed in.

The contents of her bedside table were all over the floor along with clothes from the small chest of drawers that contained her wardrobe of jeans, slogan t-shirts and dresses.

Her plain duvet was halfway off the bed and the red ceramic lamp by her bedside table was broken. There had been a struggle here.

Irrationally, I felt guilty. Perhaps if I hadn't stayed late at my shop, we could have met on time and she wouldn't have been here when the intruders entered.

I glanced at my phone, willing a message to be there telling me Aloora was at the Rummer waiting for me. Nothing. I put my phone down on her Swedish flat pack desk and began flicking through the papers left in the drawers.

There wasn't anything useful as far as I could tell. I picked my way over a stack of lacy underwear that had been strewn on the floor and started to rifle through papers there. I looked at symbols I hadn't seen before and Aloora's neat cursive handwriting next to them. I knew she translated many old languages as part of her doctorate so I wasn't surprised and none of it meant anything to me.

A symbol that looked like a person tied to a stone in red caught my eye and the word sacrifice next to it. Then, a scrawl as if Aloora had been piecing things together "*blood needed?*". I had no idea what that meant either but blood and sacrifice never sounded good together.

What had happened to Aloora? As far as I knew she wasn't mixed up in anything dodgy. Her library books were always returned on time and she was adored by her social media fans. Could one of them have done this? I wondered. She always blocked any trolls, the keyboard kind not pervy bartenders, and most of the arguments on her accounts were around the accuracy of translations rather than focusing on her.

I heard a noise outside. I grabbed the nearest thing I could find and whirled to face the door. The noise lumbered closer, accompanied by heavy breathing. I held my breath as a face appeared in the doorway, then released it in a sigh.

"Marco, thank Berathar!" I exclaimed naming the dwarven god of luck unthinkingly in my relief. Marco was one of Aloora's housemates, an English literature scholar and aspiring actor.

"What 'ave you done to Aloora's room?!" he gasped with his slight Italian accent. His hands fluttered to his chest dramatically. I sometimes wondered if those were real gestures or if his drama group membership meant he felt he had to act all the time. "And what were you going to do with that?!"

His eyes were on my hand and for the first time I looked at what I had grabbed. A plastic rounders bat that had been painted black. A prop from a Halloween costume last year when Aloora had been a zombie baseball player with grey skin and gruesome, prosthetic wounds. I had stuck to what I know and gone as a steampunk goth, not much of a stretch from my usual attire but with paler make up and copious amounts of eyeliner. There was a picture of us together at that party pinned to the cork notice board in her room. Aloora was waving her bat and both of us were making kissy faces towards the camera.

It might have looked menacing but hitting someone with a plastic bat was more likely to annoy than hurt them. I put it down on the bed, rubbing my hand on my ruined coat to get off the paint flecks that now spackled them.

"Erm, I was going to attack the intruder with it," I mumbled, realising this sounded as stupid as it looked. "And I didn't mess up her room, someone else did."

Marco raised one perfect black eyebrow and took in my torn coat and ripped legging before widening his brown eyes again.

"Your arm, it's bleeding," he stated, waving his hand towards it. "Come, come," he gestured for me to follow and I stumbled out of Aloora's room. As I nearly tripped on a pair of jeans, I noticed something glinting on the floor. I bent and picked it up carefully. It looked like a piece of jewellery, a small cut diamond in a silver leaf. The work was exquisite and clearly elven. I turned it over. There was no maker's mark or even the required hallmarks that let buyers know the quality of the metal used. I looked more closely, it wasn't silver, it was steel. There was a purple braid of silk threaded through a loop made from the stalk.

I had never seen Aloora wear anything like that. She favoured costume jewellery, big chunky rings and oversized earrings, not petite crafted charms or pendants. She also spent all her money on scrolls to help with her academic pursuits, so I couldn't imagine her finding any spare cash to spend on elven trinkets. Elven steel wasn't cheap.

As I gazed at the pendant, I felt faint magic coming from it. I didn't know what it was, but enchanted elven jewellery was expensive. I pocketed the leaf and picked up my phone before carrying on down the shabby hallway to the shared kitchen.

Marco had taken off his fashionably faded leather jacket and retrieved a first aid kit from one of the pine fronted cupboards and was setting everything out on the table in a haphazard manner. I winced at the disorder as I would have liked to straighten everything up but I appreciated the effort.

"Take your coat off," he ordered, "You need to go to….a healer or whatever you people see, but we can stitch you up for now."

I appreciated his attempt to be culturally sensitive and I fervently hoped he didn't mean literally stitch me up as I carefully took off my ruined coat.

"They're called doctors," I replied and for the first time looked properly at my own arm. My short sleeved corset top meant I didn't have to roll back any sleeves to see the wounds. There were teeth marks in my skin but the blood had slowed and they weren't as deep as I had feared.

Marco looked at me with scepticism and handed me antibacterial wipes, a bottle of water and a smaller bottle of vodka. I frowned.

"You need to clean the wound," he stated simply.

"Can you do it?" I asked hopefully.

"Ewwwww, no. I cannot stand blood."

"Can't you pretend you're in Casualty or something?"

"Yes, once it is cleaned, I will bandage it like an ER doctor," Marco drawled as he mulled over which bandages to use whilst unwinding his grey cashmere scarf from around his neck.

I sighed, bit my bottom lip in concentration and began wiping with an antibacterial wipe, wincing at the sharp sting as it touched the open wounds. Once most of the blood was off my arm, I asked for the water bottle to be opened and a towel. Marco handed me an old tea towel from a drawer. I hoped it was clean as I rested my arm on it and spilled the water into the wounds. Fresh blood, diluted with water rushed out and I grimaced.

I patted my arm dry with another towel, this one was newer and had Gryffindor written all over it. I trusted Aloora wouldn't mind me using her tea towel to clean myself. Marco unscrewed the vodka bottle and held it to me. I screwed up my face in anticipation of the pain, keeping one eye squinting so I could get the alcohol into the cuts and poured. I inhaled sharply as the vodka hit the wound and I moved to the next tooth mark.

Once I had doused myself in vodka and smelled like a student bar on a cheap shots night, I nodded to Marco. He had rolled up the sleeves on his crisp violet shirt and he nodded back, getting into his doctor role. As he began to put a large bandage over the teeth marks, I noticed a small green bottle I hadn't seen before.

"Marco, what's that?" I asked, using my good hand to point to the bottle.

"I don't know, it says *Madam Mim's Cure all* on the bottle," he mouthed the unfamiliar words carefully and held it up to me, "but no ingredients. I don't like it."

"It's a magical remedy," I replied, gritting my teeth as the vodka was still making my arm hurt. "Pour it on the wounds then pour me a shot." It looked just like my dwarven grandmother's go to medicine for everything from a cough to a graze. I knew it worked too, at least for stopping the pain and minor bleeding, having had it used on me many times when I was a child. It tasted like a mixture of mint, aniseed and whisky and I held my breath as I downed the shot Marco poured me.

Immediately I felt a warmth coursing through my body and into my arm. Marco was holding the bottle at arm's length with his nose wrinkled as he carefully allowed some drops to fall onto the open cuts. More warmth as the *Cure all* hit my skin, then the bleeding stopped.

Marco blinked in surprise, his brown eyes showing disbelief and he looked at the bottle theatrically.

"I should use this for everything!" he exclaimed.

"Yeah, yeah," I sighed. This wasn't new to me and now we were wasting time, "bandages please Dr Monzetti."

Now there wasn't any blood oozing out of my arm, Marco worked swiftly. He placed large gauzes over the cuts and stuck them down with the white tape in the first aid kit. Then he wrapped a bandage up and down my arm. I was sure he was secretly relishing playing doctor and this might get added to his CV. Once he was done, he surveyed my bruised face and the scrape down my leg.

I gestured for him to hand me the bottle and using a spare bandage, I soaked some of the *Cure All* onto it before wiping it over both. It didn't do much other than take the pain away, but that was enough.

Now I wasn't bleeding or in as much pain, I pulled the leaf I had found from my pocket.

"Have you seen this before?" I asked him, dangling it from its purple braid.

"No. Where did you find it?" He took it from me and studied it closely.

"In Aloora's room." His face screwed up as if he was trying to remember something.

"It is not hers," Marco said finally. His eyes widened again in what seemed to be his favourite expression this evening, "do you think whoever was in her room dropped it?"

"It seems that way," I hesitated before deciding to share what I knew with him. After all it wasn't much. "It's elvish and magical."

He handed it back to me quickly as if it might burn him. Then his face softened.

"Shall I take you to the hospital?" he asked. I tilted my head, considering. Marco was one of the few people I knew with a car in the city but now the *Cure All* had salved the worst of my wounds, I was keen to continue my search for Aloora. There was one bar in the city where someone might know the owner of the pendant and that was where I was going. Marco wouldn't be happy going to an all magical bar and I didn't want to have to worry about him all night.

"No, just call me a taxi, will you?" I replied.

He called a taxi and then poured me a glass of water while we waited. He waved me out when it arrived, taking care to lock the front door as I stepped into the back seat of the grey taxi. The driver looked at me nervously, noting the bandage and the rip in my trousers.

"Where to?" he asked, already pulling away from the kerb. I gave him the name of the road closest to the Royal Arcade entrance and sat back. It was tempting to shut my eyes for a moment and I forced myself to keep them open and watch the houses turn to shop fronts as we headed back towards the city centre.

Chapter 5

I paid the driver and walked towards the Royal Arcade entrance. The bright red plasterwork and white window surrounds were reflected in the orange street lights. The curved metal sign pronouncing this was Royal Arcade gleamed familiarly in the lamplight. I started unlocking the Arcade entrance on St Mary's street before he pulled away. The rain had stopped for now and the wind still bit hard as I rushed in and relocked the gate.

I made my way along the tiled floor, my footsteps echoing loudly in the silent Arcade. Normally I liked being alone here but today I was nervous and the echoes sounded uncomfortably like I was being followed.

I unlocked my shop, pulling the shutters up and opening the door cautiously. I heard something slither across the wooden floor boards and tensed before Errol came into view. I turned on the light, allowed myself to breathe again and firmly locked back up.

Errol sniffed me enthusiastically and I reached down and caressed his head. "You can smell those nasty wyrms can't you boy?"

I dropped my coat and he sniffed that too before dragging it back into his forge. I started to protest before giving up and letting him take it. Clearly he'd decided it would make a good cushion and it wasn't like I could wear it again with a massive tear in it from the wyrm attack. At least it would get some use.

I made my way up the creaky wooden steps to my flat above the shop. Flat was an aspirational word to describe my one room living area that comprised a small kitchen, double bed, small sofa, an old table with a tv and my laptop balanced on it and the cupboard that was my shower and bathroom.

Technically I shouldn't be living there, but it saved on rent and the owner of the Arcade turned a blind eye after I had solved a large rat problem for him and an even larger kobold problem with some of my dwarf friends.

I debated having a shower now, longing for hot water to massage my muscles. The digital clock on my small bedside table flashed 22:00. It felt a lot later. I decided that Aloora was more important than a shower and contented myself with a flannel wash before changing. I was quick but careful with the purple flannel as I washed around the graze on my leg and the bruises around my middle where I had hit the tarmac.

I threw the ripped leggings and corset top onto my single sage green second-hand armchair that I had bought for a bargain at a discount shop and then had been charged a small fortune for delivery and moving the heavy chair up the narrow stairs.

I picked my outfit carefully, biting my bottom lip as I considered my wardrobe. I had only been to The Goat a handful of times but the clientele were mostly magical and I wanted to both avoid unwanted attention and secure help in identifying the pendant and its owner if possible.

I decided against one of my corset tops and opted instead for sensible underwear that gave me support in case I had to flee from rogue wyrms again. Being blessed, or as I sometimes felt, cursed with large breasts, this meant a bra that was more a feat of engineering than elegant underwear underneath a v neck green jumper that would keep out the cold.

I opted for smart black jeans and kept my thick leather boots. I made a note to thank the owner of the gothic shoe shop I found them in, they had saved my feet from hungry wyrms and were still able to be worn. I dug out my thick brown sheepskin jacket, a maroon woollen scarf and matching gloves to protect me against the cold.

On an impulse, I grabbed my jewelling goggles and put them on. I stared at the pendant. It glowed slightly with a soft, whitish green glow, confirming my first thoughts that it was enchanted with elven magic. I didn't know enough about elven magic to guess at what it was enchanted to do and stuffed it securely into my pocket. I pushed the goggles on top of my head, grabbed my phone and a packet of crisps and stomped back downstairs.

I hesitated then reached behind the counter where I had stashed Bane and grabbed it. The Goat wasn't always friendly and I was going late on a Friday night. I hooked it onto my thick belt under my jacket. I didn't normally go out armed, but the axe's weight against my leg as I walked felt oddly comforting.

Errol was sat by the door, his pointed tail curled around his feet. He looked up at me expectantly.

"Go back to bed boy. You can't come tonight."

He didn't move and kept looking at me as I began to unlock the door. I thought about the bar I was going to. They let well behaved pets in from what I could remember and maybe Errol would offer me some protection if things got rough or if I was chased by strays again.

"Alright, come on then," I gave in and allowed him to climb up my uninjured arm and settle around my neck. His scales were smooth and warm and he draped himself over my shoulders in his favourite pose as I locked up again and left the arcade.

***

Errol steamed slightly in the light rain as I approached The Goat. It was a welcome refuge for magical beings who were tolerated in everyday life and every so often needed a place to let it all hang loose without fear of the Magical Liaison Office being called up.

It touted itself as an original medieval building in the city centre and black beams lay wonkily against white lime plaster. An eerie picture of a white goat with large horns stretching up was painted on a sign sticking out at an angle above the closed, heavy wooden door peppered with metal studs and a grill over a peep hole three quarters of the way up. The hole wasn't usually in use and was more for the legendary lock-ins held at the pub or, if the rumours were true, for less wholesome activities conducted out of hours.

I pulled my goggles down over my eyes and blinked as my sight adjusted through the tinted brown lenses. The Goat seemed to shimmer with light of every colour as my goggles allowed me to see the auras of magic within it. From the many different colours now visible, I ascertained there were magical beings of all types in there. Slimy green, indicating goblins by the window, a couple of blue auras for trolls and orange for orcs. There were even a number of red dwarven auras and one forest green elf aura inside.

I already knew that there would be magical beings inside so that wasn't new information. I pushed my goggles up onto my head again and straightened my back, trying to exude confidence as I strode to the door.

I grabbed the round iron handle and tugged. Nothing happened. I tried again, harder this time and Errol snorted unhappily as the effort dislodged him from his comfy spot around my neck. I sensed someone approach from behind me and turned in time to see a half-orc reaching past me.

“It’s push, love,” He sneered condescendingly as he gave the door a shove and barged past into the pub.

I glared at his back then followed him in to calls of “Close the door! It’s freezing out there!” I shoved the door shut and faced the room.

The bar was set to one side, an orc bartender working alongside a troll to dispense drinks. The lighting was muted in deference to those clients who preferred the darkness and I spied a group of goblins in the corner by the window drinking a black drink and chattering. It sounded like they were arguing but their language was quite aggressive anyway and for all I knew they could have been celebrating someone’s birthday.

The walls were maroon and dotted with framed photographs or posters of famous magical beings, often signed. I spotted one of the gorgeous elvish singer Cirian and found it hard to picture him slumming it in this bar when he wasn’t touring.

A familiar font in the picture next to it caught my eye and I recognised a small, green bottle on a faded picture with *Madam Mim’s Cure All* written on it. The attractive lady in the picture seemed to twinkle and the handwritten message marked the owner as a “dear friend”. I sent her a silent thank you for the miracle *Cure All* I’d used earlier and was suddenly accosted by a hearty slap on the back.

“Ame, my best customer! Let me buy you a drink,” I looked down into the ever optimistic smiling face of Gunther, my main supplier and one of my Dad’s friends. He was able to get any gems or metal I wanted in any quantity and was perpetually pleased to see me every time we met, although I suspected this would be the case for any of his customers.

I smiled back as he manoeuvred us past two half-orcs sitting at a small table, swigging brown drinks that looked a lot like muddy water. One of them was the male who had pushed past me to get in and he gave me a smirk as I was ushered past.

Gunther had a large square table at the back of the pub with two other dwarves I hadn't met before. They all nodded greetings as Gunther introduced me, adding "It's unusual to see you here. Mead is it?"

Despite being four foot tall, he managed to catch the bartender's eye from the table and indicated another round as I undid my jacket but kept it on, I wasn't planning on being here long. He must be a good customer because the troll immediately poured four flagons of mead and brought them over.

"Thanks Goat," said Gunther as the troll put the drinks on the table. I looked up, curious about the owner of the establishment, and Goat grunted before shuffling back to the bar.

I sipped my drink, and longed for a mug of syrupy coffee from my favourite coffee shop, the Dragon's Head, and maybe one of their brownies. I tried to enjoy the honey flavour that warmed me as I brought my attention back to Gunther.

"So, what are you doing in this neck of the woods?"

"I thought Aloora might be here. I can't find her," I was too blunt, but I wanted to get to the heart of the matter quickly. Gunther might be able to help and if I didn't focus the conversation, he might start reminiscing about Dad and one of their adolescent escapades.

"Aloora? The gnome on the internet? You know her?" Gunther's companion, Mats was suddenly interested. "Is she single?"

"Erm, yes but she's missing. Her room was ransacked and I found this, do you know who might have made it?" I pulled the pendant out of my pocket and placed it carefully on the table.

Silence fell at our table as the three dwarves looked at it carefully. Gunther pulled out an eyeglass, a jeweller's loupe, from one of his many pockets and bent over, studying it closely. He sucked in a breath.

"It's elven, of course," I nodded as he looked up at me, "and that's a pure diamond set into it," again I nodded, I'd suspected as much. "It's enchanted too."

"Do you know what kind?" I interrupted.

"Hmmm, I don't know much about elven magic, but it could be a luck enchantment."

"Or love," Mats chimed in, "This is an expensive piece, even if it is steel, perhaps a romantic gift to sweeten someone." He raised his eyebrows suggestively as he took a drink.

"Do you know who made it?" I asked him.

"There's a few elf jewellers in Britain. Elves normally prefer ivy and maple, they're big on the three parts of a leaf, but that's an oak leaf. Not a traditional design I would say… There's only one shop selling this quality of elven jewellery in Cardiff though," he added as I was about to interrupt again, "Ambrin's, in the Mall."

I had frequently passed Ambrin's when I walked through the Mall. It had a curved wooden sign and inside was polished wood and minimalist displays of select pieces hung on decorative branches. It was very expensive and definitely not my competition in the magical jewellery market.

As I mused over my next move, I was conscious that someone was standing behind me.

"Where did you get that?" asked a voice, trembling with emotion. I turned, ready to tell the newcomer to mind his own business. My eyes travelled up and up, taking in ripped jeans, the familiar sword on a thick leather belt, a dark green shirt and finally meeting his green eyes. It was the elf that had been in my shop only a few hours ago. I groaned inwardly.

"At my friend's house, she's gone missing," I replied curtly. Then I saw the anguish in his eyes behind his elven glamour and my voice softened. "Do you recognise it?"

He reached out a golden hand with long fingers as if to take it. I was still wary, despite the twinge of sympathy that I had felt and pushed my jacket aside to show my axe. I was aware of chairs scraping back and metallic chinks as the three dwarves at the table stood too. The elf thought better of taking it. He met my eyes.

"I think it belongs to my friend. May I?"

I narrowed my eyes, considering, then nodded and handed it to him. His hands were cool against my sweaty palms. I was aware of the heat of the pub making me sticky under my coat.

He lifted it to the fake candle set into a replica wrought iron sconce on the wall. The Goat really went in for olde worlde ambiance, as if that was what magical beings wanted, more stereotypes, but the pub seemed to do well enough so what did I know.

He said a word in Elvish and the pendant glowed a faint white-green colour. He put it flat on his palm and it moved, pointing towards the centre of the city. He turned, looking in the direction it pointed as if he could see through the thick walls of the pub. As he took a step towards the door, I grabbed the back of his shirt, still hanging loose though the front was neatly tucked in.

"Uh, where do you think you're going with that?" I laced my voice with sarcasm and disbelief at his arrogance.

He almost glared at me. “To find my friend.”

I shook my head and put my free hand on my axe. “Oh no. You’re going to tell me what you did to that pendant.”

He did glare at me then, and I felt a crackle of power. If it was meant to intimidate me, it failed. The dwarves moved to surround him, less subtle than I was, they had their weapons already in their hands. He noticed them and his look became almost calculating, I could see him deciding if he could take them all out and make it out of The Goat before a fight started. He shrugged, seemingly deciding that the odds were against him and then he spoke directly to me.

“Please, she might be in danger,” he pleaded.

I felt that pang of sympathy again, but judging by the state of her room, Aloora was in danger and his friend was mixed up in it.

“So is my friend. Aloora. If that thing is somehow showing you where your friend is, I’m coming too,” I stated simply, meeting his stare with an earnest gaze.

He nodded then gestured at my friends impatiently. “Can we leave now?”

Gunther looked at me. “Want us to come with you lass?” he asked in Dwarfish, shooting the elf a nasty look.

“No, I’ll be fine,” I replied with more confidence than I felt. “You stay here and I’ll call if I get in trouble.”

Gunther didn’t look like he wanted to stay, but I had his number from our frequent business transactions. He opened his mouth to argue, then shook his head as if he thought better of it.

“You’re stubborn, like your father,” he said, then smiled, “Take this,” he fished in his pocket and then pulled out a keyring. He leant towards me and pressed it into my hand that was still grabbing my axe. This meant his hand was inside my coat, as if he didn’t want the elf to see it. “It’s a charm for resistance to elvish glamour and illusion magic,” he whispered, his breath hot on my ear.

“Thank you,” I said as he leaned back and nodded to his friends. I meant it, Gunther was always able to get rare items, and I was sure this would be both valuable and effective. It might have been my imagination but the elven glamour that made them seem attractive and unattainable to other beings seemed to fade as soon as the keyring was in my possession. Annoyingly, he was still incredibly handsome even without the glamour surrounding him.

The elf had watched this exchange with a bored look, and raised one perfectly shaped eyebrow at me.

“Ready?” he asked scornfully, as if a whispered conversation with friends was beneath him. I didn’t deign to reply and instead tossed my head and stomped past him to leave the pub.

I was stopped in my tracks by a chair shoved backwards into my path. A shifter had stood violently and was beginning to growl as he turned. Sleek fur sprouting as he metamorphosed into a large black panther. The female orc sitting opposite him was weighing up a short knife, testing its balance before she threw it. He ducked and the knife slammed into the bar by my head. I froze, staring at it.

The shifter twisted, bumping me aside so hard that I fell into the bar. “Hey!” I called out. He whipped his head round to look at me, fangs dripping saliva. The elf stepped in front of me, sword drawn.

The orc had crossed the table and shoved the elf in the chest. “Stay out of it pretty boy,” her voice was low and menacing. I saw the elf’s hands start to glow as he called upon his magic. I heard voices egging the fight on and it looked like the goblins had started a gambling pool, betting on the outcome. Things were going downhill fast. Then Goat, the troll, cleared his throat. A low rumbling sound that seemed to fill the bar. He had a blunderbuss steadied by his shoulder and was pointing it at all four of us.

“Pack it in,” His words were short and simple but very effective. Magical beings healed faster than regular humans, but even a shifter would be seriously put out by being hit at nearly point blank range by the old fashioned gun.

The shifter morphed back into a human shape, only his glowing yellow eyes betraying his emotions. The female orc stepped back and put a hand on her companion’s shoulder, glaring at the elf.

“Show’s over,” stated Goat to the patrons who had been watching the fight eagerly. There were a number of groans.

“We’re leaving,” I said hastily, grabbing the elf’s sleeve and tugging him towards the door. Goat nodded and lowered the gun.

The goblins were singing a song as we finally left and a strange looking green cake had turned up at their table. Maybe they were celebrating a birthday after all.

Chapter 6

Outside, I buttoned up my sheepskin jacket against the cold wind and breathed as I waited for the elf to follow me. He didn't take long to leave behind me and with barely a glance, started striding down the street.

"Oh no," I said, grabbing his arm this time. He started to shake me off. "Look, I'm trusting you here, my best friend is missing and all I have to go on is that pendant that you're holding. I need to know what you did to it and where we're going," I paused, "and who you are and who your friend is and why she's missing and how is that related to Aloora and…" I stopped then, realising I was ranting and starting to sound hysterical.

He tilted his head, seeming to consider me, then nodded slightly with a tight smile.

"Can we walk and talk?" he asked gesturing to the street he had started to walk down.

I nodded and released his arm. "Start talking," I was curt but didn't trust myself to say more, I had been through a lot tonight and was worried for Aloora. I didn't want him to think I was a crazy woman who couldn't control her emotions, even if that might have been true.

After a couple of paces, with me almost trotting to keep up with his longer strides, the elf started talking.

"I am Lorandir. My friend is Espretha. She disappeared two days ago and I have not been able to find her," he paused, taking a deep breath and letting it out in a sigh, as if wondering how much to tell me. I kept quiet, now he was finally talking I didn't want to put him off.

"Until you walked into that pub with her pendant. She always wore it around her neck," he stopped there almost wistfully.

"What did you do to it to find her? Was it something to do with the enchantment on it?"

He glanced at me then looked ahead again. "Yes. It is a luck charm. We created it together, so I used her magical signature to locate her."

I nodded. Mats had been right, it was a luck charm but I was sure there was something else too, otherwise why couldn't he have used something else of Espretha's to locate his friend.

I had heard of 'finding magic' but had thought it was a natural gift rather than something that could be infused into jewellery. Finders were often employed by the police services for missing person cases and I knew some museums employed them when rare artworks or artefacts were stolen.

An idea popped into my head. My mind whirled with possibilities, if I could learn to infuse finding magic into my jewellery, I could market my wares as unlosable. Fuelled by the idea and possibly exhaustion, I blurted out a question.

"Can anyone do that?"

Lorandir looked shocked. I clarified and modified my tone to one of mild interest, "I've never heard of finding someone with an artefact, unless you're a natural finder?"

He seemed to think about it for a long while and I forced myself to stay silent too, as we continued towards wherever he thought Espretha was.

"It is a, I think the word would be, 'friend' charm in English. Elves form these with special… friends, I think is the word, who they have a lifelong bond with. It allows us to contact each other."

"Like a phone?" I asked, before realising that sounded sarcastic.

"No," he sounded exasperated, "more like a connection. We can sense each other's emotions and know if the other is in trouble. When this was torn from her neck, I lost that connection and knew she was in trouble but I couldn't find it or her. It was like it was cloaked with other magic. It's hard to explain."

I thought back to Aloora's room. There was always a slight magical energy coming from it but as it reminded me of her, I had never really thought about it before.

"Aloora has a lot of magical scrolls," I spoke my thoughts aloud, "perhaps one of them was cloaking it or blocking the magic somehow."

He glanced at me again; he looked a little impressed with my logic. Then his eyes squinted slightly as if remembering something.

"Aloora…do you mean Aloora Dragonquest?" he asked, using her online handle.

"That's her," I didn't say anything else. People often recognised Aloora and she enjoyed her lively debates on social media. I expected him to be star struck or start quizzing me about her latest posts, but he simply nodded as if it was normal to be searching for a minor social media celebrity on a Friday night.

We didn't talk much for the rest of the journey as he strode and I practically jogged across the city to our destination. The city was remarkably quiet, the only figures we saw were vampires and donors crowded around the all night blood store. I gave an involuntary shudder as we passed the Capitol Shopping Centre with its modern neon sign for 'B', glowing red, of course. We hurried on past the disinterested queues.

He paused outside a tower block of sleek apartments near the railway line and we both looked up, the building seeming to reach to the sky. The concrete looked formidable in the night and the sheer glass windows were mostly dark with only a few shining brightly to indicate occupants were home.

"She's in there," his voice shook slightly and I knew he was anxious. So was I. That pang of sympathy tugged at my chest again. On a whim, I pulled my goggles over my eyes and looked up. There weren't many magical auras that I could see, a couple of half trolls close by, on the first floor I guessed. I continued to look up, craning my neck and disturbing Errol, who snorted unhappily and dug his claws into my coat in protest. It was a tall building so I could have been mistaken, but it looked like there were a couple of forest green elf auras and several violet gnomish auras, although I couldn't work out how many or how high up they were from this angle.

I pushed the goggles back onto my head and scanned the metal buttons on the entrance pad. There was a code to get in. There was also another pad of numbers to the right of the door that connected to a speaker. This was clearly how visitors got buzzed in.

"Any idea which flat she's in?" I asked hopefully but wasn't surprised when he shook his head, his mane of blonde hair catching in the wind and blowing into his face. I supressed a smile at seeing a dishevelled elf and pressed two numbers at random.

I heard the digital beeps that indicated a buzzer was ringing somewhere in the building but it ended after five rings. I wasn't surprised. The few windows lit up suggested there weren't many people in or awake this evening and it was late. I tried again and this time someone picked up after two rings.

"Who is it?" asked a nasally voice through the speaker. I looked at the elf, who shrugged unhelpfully.

"Er, pizza delivery?" I said tentatively.

"Where's the boxes? And I didn't order a pizza." Damn, there must be a camera. I should have expected that in this expensive a building. The speaker hung up. They might be calling the police as we waited.

I studied the digital pad by the entrance. I had my unlocking key on me, but I had only ever used it for locks at the Arcade and my own shop, not on keypads. It was worth a go I supposed. I took it out of my pocket and placed it near the keypad. Open, I thought, willing it to work.

To my surprise the door clicked and I pushed, opening it all the way. I put my key away carefully, and looked behind me towards Lorandir.

"Well come on then," I gestured, pushing the door open confidently as if breaking and entering was something I did regularly.

We stood on the clean, white tiles of the foyer and I let the door clank shut behind us. The noise echoed through the empty lobby. Luckily there were no security guards here.

Lorandir glanced up and slightly to the left. He waved vaguely. "She's up there."

"I don't suppose you can tell which floor, can you?" I asked hopefully.

He shook his head. I walked to the lift and stepped in as it opened almost immediately. “Guess we’re going to have to stop on every floor then,” I said cheerily as I mashed all the buttons making them light up.

He sighed and stepped in. My stomach rolled slightly as the lift lurched upwards. Errol hissed softly. He didn’t enjoy the lift any more than I did. It was only a few seconds before we were at the first floor and my stomach rolled again as the lift jerked to a stop. I gazed expectantly at Lorandir as the doors opened.

He shook his head, looked upwards and stayed put. I sighed. This was going to be a long lift ride. I started humming a tune as I looked around the metal box we were riding in, trying to ignore the small lurches in my stomach every time the lift stopped and started. Lorandir glared at me. I met his eyes and hummed a little louder, not caring if it offended his elvish ears. I saw his jaw tighten but he stayed silent and his gaze drifted upwards again, towards Espretha.

On the tenth floor, Lorandir stopped looking upwards and looked forwards and to the left.

“Here?” I asked tensely. The constant stopping and starting of the lift had put me on edge and I didn’t know what we were walking towards.

Lorandir nodded. He seemed to be tense too. We stepped cautiously out of the lift and the metal doors slid silently shut behind us. I pulled on my goggles and looked to the right. Several violet auras were in one of the flats, a gnomish family perhaps, but Aloora hadn’t mentioned relatives in the city, so I guessed she wasn’t with them. I looked to the left and saw a couple of forest green auras and one pale violet one. My heart jumped to my stomach; that could be her. I pointed in that direction and Lorandir started walking slowly down the corridor to the left. Being an elf, his steps were light and the plush blue carpet muffled my steps as I followed behind.

The goggles made it dark inside so I pushed them back up on my head, wincing as they caught a strand of hair. I considered the modern artwork dotted throughout the hall as we walked. The elf paused by every door then continued until he reached the very end of the corridor. At the last grey door, opposite a painting that was called "Summer Sun" but could equally have been called "Expensive Blobs of Yellow on Bright Blue", he stopped and looked at me.

"She's in there," he put his ear to the door, "I can hear voices but not what they're saying."

I moved one of my plaits out of the way and pressed my ear to the door. I could hear mumbling too. Errol stirred on my shoulders, sniffing. He loved Aloora because she always brought beef jerky for him whenever she came over to my place. "What can you smell boy? Is Aloora in there?" I petted his head soothingly. I pulled the goggles back down and immediately saw two very bright forest green auras and a paler violet one off to the left, in a different room perhaps.

"Two elves and a gnome are in there," I confirmed in a whisper. "What's the plan?" Lorandir met my eyes with a surprised look. We had come all this way and he didn't have a plan.

"We knock and ask if they've seen Espretha and Aloora."

"Right," I replied, "and then?"

"What do you want to do?" he hissed back at me. "Break the door down? We don't know who is in there. What if there are children?"

I started. I hadn't considered this could just be a family having a late movie night with some magical guests, my goggles didn't sense humans after all. I didn't have a better plan.

"OK, OK," I said, raising my hands in an appeasing gesture, "but if they don't answer…"

"We'll cross that bridge when we come to it," Lorandir replied with finality. Great, I thought, but I nodded. I fingered the key in my pocket, we could get in if we needed to.

Lorandir lifted his hand and knocked sharply on the grey door. I stayed slightly to the left of the door out of sight of the peephole drilled at average human height in the door. If it was his friend, all well and good but if it was something more sinister then the element of surprise wouldn't hurt. Errol scrabbled down my body and sat at attention by my feet. He was very alert and I felt a surge of hope that we had indeed found Aloora.

There was a long pause as we waited but then I heard footsteps moving towards the door. The sound of the peephole shutter being lifted and then muffled voices.

Lorandir cleared his throat then knocked again. I gripped Bane and tensed, prepared for trouble. To my surprise, the door opened slightly and light flowed out into the hallway.

"Espretha!" Lorandir exclaimed, emotion making his voice crack. "You're all right. I was so worried."

Espretha cut him off. "What are you doing here?" She sounded nervous and slightly pissed off rather than pleased to see him. "You have to go," she made to shut the door.

Lorandir put his hand on it, resisting slightly. "Please. What's happening? Are you alright?"

"You have to go," Espretha repeated. As she made to shut the door, Errol darted forward and squeezed through the opening. Espretha gave a shriek as if she had seen a mouse and released the door, which swung open.

Lorandir stood there looking baffled. I stepped forward and Espretha shrieked again as she saw me, and I barged through the now open door and into the short corridor.

Inside were white walls and pale laminate flooring, modern and easy to maintain. “Errol,” I called, trying to sound sure of myself when I’d pushed my way into someone’s home.

I made it to the open plan living space, a white leather sofa facing a sleek tv screen and, behind that, floor to ceiling windows showing a view over the city. The skyline was lit up with street lights glowing against the dark night sky and some sort of laser show going on above one of the clubs in what I guessed was the direction of Cardiff Bay.

A picture hung above an electric fireplace which was heating the flat, with fake flames flickering above smooth white pebbles. It was so large and out of place in such a modern building that it drew my eye.

In contrast with the modern canvas artwork in the shared hallway, this picture was in an ornate golden frame and had a medieval or renaissance look to it. It showed a large red dragon reared up fiercely with its jaws open, breathing fire at several silhouetted people who were cowering. It struck me as an odd choice of picture for this flat.

A dark-haired elf was standing in the kitchen. He wasn’t happy about a dwarf barging into his home and had picked up a large knife. I held up my hands in a gesture of peace.

Espretha seemed to have regained her composure as she entered the room. Lorandir was loitering sheepishly in the hallway. He had expected her to be in trouble but it looked like she was shacking up with another elf without telling him.

The male elf looked at her with meaning and I wondered if elves were telepathic.

"You need to leave," she stated, clearly shifting her gaze to me and looking me up and down as if I was a piece of dirt. I glared back, but there wasn't really a good reason to be in her home if she was fine.

"Of course," I replied in a sickly-sweet voice, "As soon as I find Errol," I added with some satisfaction as her narrow lips pursed and her large blue eyes narrowed. With Gunther's charm, I wasn't affected by elvish glamour but they were still beautiful.

At this point, I heard a scuffling sound and turned to the source. Errol was scratching frantically at a closed wooden door on the same wall as the fireplace and the weird painting. The hairs on the back of my neck stood up. This was unusual behaviour.

I walked to the door, and made to open it.

"NO!" screamed Espretha. I turned to look at her. What was behind that door?

The dark-haired elf looked at her then shrugged and threw the kitchen knife towards me. I ducked just in time. It thudded into the wood of the door. I glanced up, it was embedded up to the hilt; the elf was strong.

I drew Bane and stood again, switching to what I hoped was an intimidating dwarven battle stance. The male elf's hands were now glowing an electric blue as he summoned magic. I dived behind the sofa as he launched the spell; I didn't want to chance Gunther's charm not working. I felt the heat of the spell and the sofa shuddered as it took the brunt of the blow.

Espretha had turned and drawn a curved knife with a bone handle, that I hadn't seen her carrying. She stabbed wildly towards Lorandir. He gracefully side stepped her attack and ducked under her arm into the living room where he finally drew his sword. I heard him mutter "Sheld" in passable Dwarfish as he joined me behind the sofa.

The male elf launched another magic attack, which this time bounced off Lorandir's enchanted shield. I took a moment to have pride in my craft. It wasn't often I saw weapons I had forged in battle, and the protection charm was working well, thank goodness.

"What's the plan?" I asked Lorandir out of the side of my mouth. This time he had an answer.

"Can you sneak around to the kitchen if I distract them?" he asked. I nodded slightly with my head.

I tensed, ready to launch myself towards the kitchen. Lorandir murmured something under his breath and extended his arm towards the window. A deafening crash sounded and cold wind suddenly whipped into the room. It turned out his distraction was blowing the windows out.

Both Espretha and the male elf were surprised by this. In the instant that they turned to duck, I rolled and scurried in a crab-like crouch to the kitchen counter. I was hidden from the male elf, who I desperately hoped hadn't seen me. If Espretha looked in this direction, I was clearly visible.

I took a breath, grabbed Bane with both hands and stepped out from behind the counter. I was now the same side as the male elf. His sharp eyes spotted my movement immediately and he grabbed another knife from an open drawer in front of him. This one was a cleaver and it looked like he knew how to use it.

I dodged his first swipe by stepping backwards. I swung Bane towards his stomach as he moved to follow me. He retreated and I pressed my advantage. Bane was double-headed so I didn't have to worry about turning the axe and instead I reversed my swing, again aiming for his stomach. He parried with the knife and then turned his parry into an attack.

I had done some battle-axe training with my family, what dwarf hadn't? My Dad had been determined that I could at least handle the ancestral axe but this elf was another level. Somehow I fought by instinct or perhaps Bane helped, fuelled by previous battle experience. I managed to block the magic user's attacks.

As he pressed forward, I saw an opening. He was fighting as if I was a warrior. I was not. I blocked his next blow then ran towards him, moving inside his reach. I was stocky and my weight took him off balance. I shoved him. I went down with him, landing heavily on his chest and winding him. His eyes had a slightly panicked look as he'd been expecting to win easily.

I knelt, digging my knee into his groin and taking some satisfaction from his groan of pain as he instinctively tried to curl up.

I hit his hand with the flat of my axe. He dropped the cleaver with another gasp of pain. I raised myself upwards, placing my boot on his neck in case he tried anything. As I stood, I could see over the counter.

Espretha and Lorandir were fighting. It was strange to watch, as she couldn't get through the magical barrier created by my charm. He was able to attack, but I could see he was careful not to injure her. He was fighting to disarm her. She looked a lot more desperate as she lunged at him. Errol was still scratching at the door, smoke curling from his nostrils.

As I was distracted by the fight in the living space, the elf grabbed my boot with both hands and pushed hard. For someone so slim, he had surprising strength and I felt my leg move upwards, taking me off balance. As I whirled my arm to grab the counter, a blast of magic took me. I cursed and gritted my teeth as I tried desperately to grab something.

The magic wasn't hurting, it was as if a gust of wind was trying to push me. I didn't know if it was Gunther's charm or my natural low centre of gravity, but it was like being battered by a very strong wind. Judging by the elf's expression of concentration, it was meant to do more than that. I felt the strength increase as he put more effort into the spell. I abandoned my attempt to grab something and instead dived forward, flattening myself to the floor.

My plan partially worked but as I was heading to the floor, the wind took me. It carried me towards the destroyed window. The elf was standing now, his arms outstretched, focusing all of his power on me.

I called out in fury and desperation, trying to push back as my feet connected with the ground. My plaits were flapping behind me and I felt like I was trying to walk in a tornado.

I looked at Lorandir. He was still fighting Espretha but had been alerted to my distress by my cry. Errol also seemed to have been roused from his door and he slunk behind Espretha and sunk his teeth into her calf. She screamed, and turned to face this new threat, trying to kick him off.

Lorandir used Errol's distraction to hurl a blast of magic at my tormentor. The dark-haired elf staggered off balance as my shoes reached the edge of the kitchen floor. I managed to take a few steps forward, but then my attacker shot another blast at me. I was swept off my feet, hitting the laminate floor hard. I was winded and now moving along the floor. I felt my feet hang over thin air and frantically tried to commando crawl forward back into the room.

The elf snarled, "Stop or I will finish her!"

Lorandir stopped mid step on his way towards the kitchen. The dark-haired elf stepped backwards, his eyes flicking from me to Lorandir.

I tried to wriggle forwards but was held by firmly in place by the magic.

Espretha had managed to kick Errol off and picked him up behind his head, holding him at arm's length so his claws couldn't find purchase. She moved to the hallway and stood alongside the male elf.

As they stared at us, Errol managed to turn his body and gouged Espretha's arm. She screamed and released him, grabbing her injured arm. I noted with irony, that it was the same side that I had injured earlier in a very different wyrm attack. That felt like a year ago. Errol snorted fire and her tight indigo jeans began to smoulder. She shrieked and batted at them frantically with her other arm.

"Let's go!" she shouted hysterically to her friend. He scrunched up his mouth, twisting his attractive face into a scowl. Then he looked directly at Lorandir.

"Chase us or save her. Your choice," with that, the elf blasted me with more magic and I slid backwards.

I cursed in Dwarfish as I felt my body hang over nothing, my legs kicked uselessly and my hands scrabbled to find something to hold onto. I managed to grab a piece of glass that was jutting upwards in the frame, somehow surviving the earlier blast. It cut my hands and I felt blood trickling down my wrist but I hung on. My life depended on it.

I felt a strong hand grab my wrist and looked away from the glass and into Lorandir's face. He grunted and braced himself before beginning to hoist me upwards. He was stronger than I expected from his slim build. It felt like an eternity but in reality was only a few seconds before I fell awkwardly on top of him as he finished pulling me in.

I lay there for three heartbeats with my eyes closed, enjoying being alive but not fully believing I was safe in the flat. In that moment, everything seemed more real than ever. The air in my lungs felt new and fresh, my body felt warm and alive. It was the adrenaline coursing through me and it felt good.

He coughed and I opened my eyes, meeting his.

"Thank you," I gasped.

"Not at all," he replied without any arrogance. I pushed myself up, leaving bloody handprints on the floor as I heaved myself off him. I offered him my hand but he gave it a haughty look and clambered upright with a lot more grace than I had. He considered me.

"You're hurt," he said and had the good grace to look embarrassed as I stared at him for stating the obvious. Before I could say anything else, he reached for my hand and his palm started glowing with a soft gold aura. As he touched me, I felt his power enter my hand and travel up my arm which was still not fully healed from the wyrm attack earlier that evening.

I had never been healed by magic before, *Madam Mim's Cure All* aside. It was a strange sensation, a sort of tingling warmth that started with my hand where Lorandir touched me and continued through my body. When it found a cut or bruise, there was more intense heat but it wasn't painful. I closed my eyes and felt for his power. I wasn't particularly sensitive to elven magic but somehow I had an impression of trees, their leaves golden in summer sunlight and the taste of soft honeyed mead and dark, bittersweet chocolate. It felt like hours but I suppose it was only seconds before I was aware of the warmth of his power leaving me, retreating back through my now healed body and leaving via my palm, which Lorandir was still holding.

I opened my eyes and immediately felt dizzy, feeling the absence of his magic. He eyed me with concern as I swayed slightly but said nothing.

Errol was now whining loudly, his sharp claws had already destroyed the finish on the corner of the polished door. I glanced at Lorandir then walked over. I put my hand on the silver handle, nodded to the elf and wrenched the door open as Lorandir stepped through brandishing his sword. I heard a muffled shriek as if someone was trying to scream through a pillow and followed him in cautiously.

As my eyes adjusted to the dark room, after the electric light in the kitchen cum living space, I saw a small form huddled on a large bed. I flipped the light switch by the door and couldn't help sighing and rushing over when I saw my friend on the bed. She was frantically kicking the sheets, focused on Lorandir, or more accurately, on his sword when I landed on the bed and pulled her into a hug. The soft mattress dipped at my weight and I tried to breathe and not let the sobs I was feeling fill me.

Aloora made some odd noises and I broke off the hug and looked at her properly. Tears were running down her face. A green gag had been stuffed in her mouth and I fumbled to untie it, trying to soothe her as I did so. Once it was out she took deep noisy sobs and I held her, stroking her spiky hair.

Lorandir was kneeling by the bed and was trying to undo the handcuffs that secured her to the iron bedframe. He didn't have any joy and stood, taking a step back and aiming his sword. I saw what he was about to do and stepped off the bed in alarm. He might be a good swordsman but there was no way I was risking Aloora's hands to his aim.

"Let me try!" I shouted, my voice sounding louder than I expected in the quiet room, with an edge of panic that stemmed from concern for my best friend. Lorandir looked at me with confusion and I studiously ignored him as I took my unlocking key out of my pocket and pressed it to the handcuffs. Although it didn't fit into the small hole, it seemed to work as I heard a soft click and was able to undo the cuffs and free Aloora.

"Are you hurt Ally?" I asked her anxiously as she rubbed her wrists.

"No…well my hands hurt, but I'm OK," she started to shake, "I'm sorry, I…"

"Shhhh," I cut her off, "you have no need to apologise."

Aloora started to stand and I supported her with one arm around her waist and the other holding her hand closest to me. As we walked out into the stark, white living area, I suddenly noticed the mess.

"Schiztz!" I exclaimed, "How are we going to explain this?"

Lorandir looked lazily around the room as if taking it in for the first time.

"We could just go…" he trailed off.

I snorted. "My blood is everywhere and Aloora was attacked and kidnapped. We need to call the police," I heard sirens in the distance, "if someone hasn't already," I muttered.

I took out my phone and made the call, asking for an ambulance for Aloora as well as the police, even though she insisted she was alright. Then I made a second call to Marco to reassure him that I'd found his flatmate and a third to Gunther. He must have been waiting for me to call as he picked up on the first ring. I briefly filled him in, leaving out the part about being flung over the edge of the building. It still made me queasy thinking about it. I told him not to come before hanging up, as he protested loudly at the other end of the phone.

Now that we weren't trying to leave the flat quickly, I decided to make some tea. Aloora was still shaking and the massive hole where the window had been was letting in the cold wind.

The police arrived quickly, confirming my suspicion that they had already been alerted by the explosion or the fighting. They took statements from each of us and looked very surprised at the account, noting the shattered glass, my blood and the handcuffs. They called an ambulance so that Aloora could be checked out properly, and I accompanied her on the journey, bumping around in the padded spare seat and trying to keep myself and Errol out of the way of the efficient medic who was taking readings from a very pale looking Aloora.

When we arrived at the hospital, I found that Lorandir had followed us in a cab and without a word he tailed us inside. He was silent while we waited in the emergency waiting room and I leant back in the uncomfortable plastic chair, noting the time. Three am. I was tired and kept yawning. Errol closed his eyes and tuned out the beeping of the medical equipment and was soon snoring, softly curled around my neck. I was thankful that the medical staff tactfully ignored him as Aloora was finally called and taken to be looked at.

After prodding and poking her, they decided she needed to stay in for observation, whatever that meant, and settled her into a bed. As she was a referral from the police, she got her own room and it hurt to see her in the hospital bed with a tube sticking out of her thin arm.

"You should go home," she mumbled as she fought sleep.

I harrumphed. "Not likely, what if someone tries to hurt you again?"

Lorandir had crept into the room too. Even he had light blue smudges under his eyes, though they didn't diminish his attractiveness. If the elf looked like that, I must look terrible, I thought, as I brushed hair off my face, then lowered my hand quickly as Errol shifted. Wyrms were a grey category in the pet area and I was surprised no one had tried to make him wait outside but as he could technically sterilise himself with his fire and I had heard rumours that the university hospital was using magical creatures to help their research, I kept quiet and said nothing.

"You're too tired to do anything," replied Aloora with her eyes shut. "Go home."

My friend was always sensible. I racked my brains for a smart response but realised she was right. I needed sleep and we needed to talk about what had happened, but that would have to wait. I sighed then called Gunther. I trusted him and he was good with an axe. He would help.

As I waited for my friend to show, I snuck a look at Lorandir. He was sitting in a plastic chair, looking relaxed and comfortable. His eyes were shut and his face looked serene. I studied his perfect cheekbones and wondered what he was still doing here. He could have gone once his friend had left him, but he had stayed, staring unseeing into the distance until he fell asleep. I wondered what was going through his mind after he found out his childhood friend was a kidnapper and partnered with a would-be killer. I decided not to ask, I didn't want to disturb him and I was a little afraid of what the answer might be.

Gunther arrived barely an hour later and after a very brief exchange, which awakened the elf but fortunately not Aloora who needed sleep. I gave him my seat next to Aloora's bed and left with Lorandir in my wake.

I yawned many times as we walked the empty cold corridors which had a tinge of blue thanks to the reflection of the lights on the floor. I hated hospitals and was glad to be leaving but I shivered as we left. I blinked in the strange pre-dawn light. The rain from the previous night had vanished and instead a swirling mist encased the car park, giving the grey tarmac an ethereal feel. I rubbed my eyes before I saw a taxi waiting and got in. Errol was still asleep and the driver didn't seem to notice him so I didn't have to argue, which was a bonus as I wasn't sure I had the energy to convince the driver he wasn't a danger, and I definitely didn't want to walk home from the hospital on the outskirts of Cardiff.

Lorandir followed me into the slightly stained back seat of the car and I didn't have the energy to question him as I gave the driver my address and then leaned back, closing my eyes as we turned onto the main road and started back to the closest street to my workshop cum house.

Chapter 7

The drive back was mercifully uneventful or at least I suppose it was as I was asleep for most of it. I paid the fare and was dimly aware of Lorandir climbing out of the grey, Cardiff taxi after me and following me home.

We made it to the Arcade, which was still locked as it was only just dawn. I fumbled with my key and opened the thick metal gate.

I turned, "Well, this is me…"

Lorandir nodded simply. Obviously he knew where I lived; he had heard me give my address to the taxi driver and had been in my shop only yesterday. Sleep deprivation was clearly affecting me.

"Err, you can come in if you want, I'll make some breakfast," I added lamely. I held my breath hoping he'd leave as I opened the gate and walked through.

"Thank you," he replied. Schiztz, I thought but I plastered a smile on my face as I walked to the shop. Errol jumped off my shoulders as soon as we got inside and raced to his forge, either to grab some coal to eat or to sleep some more.

Lorandir followed me inside and upstairs. Part of me really wanted to tell him to get lost, but he had helped me find Aloora and healed me and he'd just found out his friend didn't want him anymore. I was glad my living space was tidy, even with my destroyed clothes flung over a chair.

I sat on the small sofa, sinking into the cushions and closed my eyes, intending to rest for a moment before cooking us an omelette. I was dimly aware of Lorandir seating himself next to me.

The next thing I knew, I was blinking awake. I glanced to my right and saw Lorandir sleeping on the sofa, his head at an uncomfortable angle on the cushions but otherwise looking annoyingly unruffled considering what we had been through last night. I allowed myself a smile as he was going to wake up with a crick in his neck. I slipped my phone out of my pocket and grimaced when I noticed the time. I'd been asleep for hours…with a strange man in my house…who I had invited in for breakfast!

My stomach growled and I lurched in embarrassment. I hadn't eaten properly since lunch time yesterday, one bowl of chips and a packet of crisps barely counted, so it was understandable but as Lorandir blinked, I was mortified that my stomach had managed to wake someone up. He seemed surprised at his surroundings because he looked round before resting his gaze on me. He gave me a lopsided smile then winced, putting his hand to his neck.

I pretended not to notice and stood up too quickly, pushing away the light-headedness as I walked the few steps to my small kitchen.

"Omelette?" I asked over my shoulder, hoping the elf wasn't vegan and mentally going through my cupboards to see if I had anything vegan in the kitchen. I had an orange, a few vegetables and some pasta, and I wasn't 100% sure pasta was vegan.

"Please," he replied sleepily, "Can I help?"

I shook my head and concentrated on preparing the omelettes, taking out my good omelette frying pan, which was my only frying pan but

I had got it for the online omelette-making reviews. I like organisation in the kitchen. Aloora would say I have a mild obsession when it comes to cooking, but I always chop everything first onto separate plates before even starting to cook. It's less about being tidy and more about being paranoid I might poison someone.

I trimmed a little of the home-grown greyish-green mushrooms I had on the shelf above the sink, when I heard a gasp behind me. I turned quickly, my hand gripping the kitchen knife when I saw it was Lorandir with a disbelieving look on his face.

"Is that Mucklewhite?" he asked

"Yeees," I wondered where this was going.

"I haven't had fresh Mucklewhite in ages and Gundersson's always charges a fortune for the dried stuff," he paused and gave a snort, "I didn't know dwarves were gardeners," he added, the thought obviously tickling him.

"What about the French pleasure gardens?" I retorted defensively, naming one of the most famous feats of dwarfish engineering landscaping that I knew of.

He considered my point and replied with sincerity, "Apologies, I had forgotten dwarves *are* amazing landscape artists."

I relaxed and snorted. "Some dwarves might be but I am not," I gestured to the mushrooms and the pots of soil next to them, relics of previous house plants. "My mum keeps buying me plants in the hope that one day I'll be able to grow something. These Mucklewhite mushrooms are the only things I haven't managed to kill…yet."

I sprinkled some into the pan to mix with the eggs, ham, cheese and peppers I had already added from their separate bowls, and let it cook all the way through. Once I was happy it was cooked, I tipped the omelette onto a plain white plate and passed it to him. The only table I had was holding my tv and laptop so he had to eat on his lap. Annoyingly, he still managed to do this gracefully. I opted to stand and eat my omelette leaning on the small kitchen counter.

"Thank you, this is delicious," Lorandir said between bites. I scanned the comment for sarcasm but couldn't find any so I simply nodded.

"You're welcome. Thank you again for saving my life."

"You're welcome. I'll have to do it more often if you cook like this," he raised his fork slightly and took another bite with a smile. I scrunched up my face, what did he mean save my life more often? I decided it was meant to be a joke so I smiled back and carried on eating. Bloody elves.

After we had eaten, I checked my phone. There were no new updates so I messaged Gunther asking how Aloora was. He replied immediately.

She's sleeping. Still in hospital. A guy called Marco is here, he says he's her flatmate...should I let him in?

I knew Gunther had been a good choice to call, he was steadfast and protective, even if he hardly knew Aloora.

Yes, let him in. Let me know if anything changes. Thanks for the charm, it worked great. x

I pressed send before I realised the kiss was probably a mistake. Gunther replied with a smiley face and I let Lorandir know Aloora was still in hospital. He gazed at a spot on my magnolia coloured wall, as if he was thinking about something else.

I left him to it. He'd just found out his friend was a kidnapper after all. I started to go downstairs. If he'd wanted to hurt me or steal anything he'd had ample opportunity while I was asleep. I wasn't entirely comfortable with him staying in my flat but it was Saturday and I should open my shop. On the first step, I suddenly realised I hadn't showered since the fight and probably looked a mess.

"I'm going to shower," I announced, too loudly. I hurriedly grabbed some clothes and shut myself into the converted cupboard that was my shower and bathroom combined. I turned on the shower, hung my clothes on the door and stepped into the hot water. I shut my eyes. It was all too much. My best friend was in hospital, I'd been attacked by wyrms and elves and now there was an elf in my home. I sunk to the floor and allowed myself two minutes of crying in the shower where I was sure even the low pressured water would cover the sound of any sobbing then washed quickly and stepped out. I was glad this adventure was over and I could get back to normal.

I checked the door was still locked, I was becoming paranoid, before drying and dressing quickly and dragging a brush through my hair. A glance at the mirror confirmed that I looked presentable and I rubbed my eyes, wishing as always that they were a more vibrant colour than mud-brown. The lack of sleep had made them puffy and I swept some green eyeshadow on to try to brighten them and some pink lip gloss before stepping out.

Lorandir seemed uncomfortable as I left the bathroom, leftover steam escaping into the room.

"Err, can I use the bathroom?" he asked eventually. I almost laughed at the haughty elf asking permission for anything but stopped myself in time.

"Of course. There should be hot water left," he still seemed hesitant and I realised he didn't have anything with him, except his clothes and a sword. I grabbed a clean towel from a small wicker chest just outside the bathroom and threw it to him. He caught it deftly before it hit his face.

"I'm going to open the shop," I announced then stomped downstairs and left him to it. It was early afternoon and there were still plenty of people in the Arcade as I opened up my shop and settled behind the shabby chic counter after checking on Errol. The wyrm blinked at me as if to say *how dare you wake me*, as I opened the door to the forge but soon became more eager to see me as I poured fresh coal into his bowl and scratched him behind his ears, enjoying the warmth that emanated from him.

I sold a silver bracelet and a pair of earrings to a mother looking for a birthday present for her daughter to make up for not being there on the actual day. I was in the process of packaging up two friendship charms and a love charm to a pair of teenage girls who giggled as they bought it before Lorandir emerged. He walked down the steps with natural grace, still wearing his sword, and the teenage girls sniggered even more when they saw him, whispering something to each other and gesturing at me. To my horror, I felt myself blushing, a dark red creeping up my chest to my face. Lorandir must have heard what they said with his sensitive hearing because he gave me a wink and smiled flirtatiously at them.

I frowned at his back; he had just found out his lifelong friend was a kidnapper and he was flirting. Bloody elves, so keen on keeping up appearances.

The girls looked like they were about to faint so I asked them if they wanted anything else. Unable to think of an excuse to stay, they left, giggling explosively as they passed the window on the way to the next shop.

"Cul," I muttered under my breath.

"What?" Lorandir asked. Damn his elvish hearing.

"Er, coffee?" I asked brightly.

He narrowed his eyes but replied civilly. "Tea, if you have it?"

I made us both a cup with the kettle I kept in my forge, dodging Errol as he wound his way around my legs while I made two cups of strong and milky tea, just how I liked it. His eyebrow quirked up at the Little Miss Sunshine mug I gave him. Mum had bought it for me in a fit of irony during my surly teenage years when I had been the opposite of a ray of sunshine to live with. I kept my favourite mug with a picture of a cute red dragon on it that reminded me of Errol.

I was about to ask him what he was planning to do now when another customer entered the shop. The man had a faint magical aura about him, but I couldn't tell more than that without my goggles. I guessed he was half or quarter magic-blood and given his rugby player build, I thought he was probably part-orc. He looked at Lorandir then me, then back to Lorandir and asked him for advice choosing a present for his girlfriend before I had time to open my mouth for my opening spiel. Typical.

Lorandir shot me a look and I raised an eyebrow at him.

"I think this is exquisitely crafted," he said smoothly, pointing at one of my pricier necklaces set with a small purple amethyst. I always enjoyed crafting with my namesake stone and this one was set into a complex pattern of entwining golden vines symbolising eternity. "But you should ask the owner, she makes them." I was taken aback as he pointed to me.

The customer was clearly taken aback too but he switched on a dazzling smile. "It's beautiful," he agreed, "how much?"

I walked over to both of them, feeling very small as they both towered over me by more than a foot. I unlocked the cabinet and held the necklace up so it caught the light and glinted. I named the price.

He seemed unsure and I was about to put it back when Lorandir added without a trace of irony, “Perhaps you would like the lady to model it?”

I wanted to respond furiously but aware of the potential sale, I forced a smile onto my face and nodded. “If you would like, sir?” I added for good measure, it always helped to be polite.

The man nodded. I fumbled with the catch unprofessionally and Lorandir stepped forward. “Allow me,” I kept the smile plastered on my face as he stepped uncomfortably close and tucked my braids out of the way before placing the necklace over my head and around my neck. I wished I had chosen a polo neck jumper, but my wardrobe consisted of a lot of steampunk inspired clothes and I had a fitted v neck shirt on, which complemented my figure but felt like it exposed entirely too much skin when an elf was brushing my shoulders. His fingers felt cool against my blushing skin as he held it there while the customer contemplated the golden necklace with a considering look.

After what seemed like an eternity of myself and my craft being examined, the man nodded. “I’ll take it,” he said with relief. “I’ve been looking for the perfect present for ages,” he continued chatting as I took the necklace from Lorandir and placed it in a gift box and one of the light turquoise bags that proclaimed “Amethyst’s Treasures” in shiny purple lettering.

I smiled as he left the shop, then glared at Lorandir, who was looking very smug.

“I never knew I was good at retail,” he remarked with satisfaction, “perhaps we should work together more often…”

I spluttered at the suggestion and was about to respond with a snide remark when my phone rang. I fumbled to get it out of my pocket. I held one finger out to let Lorandir know that we were pausing that conversation while I answered.

"Aloora!" It was a relief to hear her voice. I frowned as she asked me to come over in an anxious voice before I could ask if she was alright.

"Of course I'll come. Give me a minute to shut up the shop and I'll come straight over. Are you OK?" My worry turned to confusion as she ignored my question and asked me if the elf was still with me.

"Yes he's still here," I said pointedly, glaring at Lorandir who smiled blandly then returned to casually regarding one of my cases of charms as if he wasn't listening.

"OK, yes I'll bring him. Yeah we'll leave now. See you soon, take care."

"Are we going somewhere?" he asked mildly once I'd hung up as if he hadn't been listening.

"Aloora's back home," I replied curtly, "she wants to see you." I was a little hurt she wanted to see the elf but chided myself internally. The important thing was she was OK and out of hospital.

He nodded as if it was normal for complete strangers to want to see him. "Are we walking or driving?"

"Do you have a car?" I was only slightly sarcastic as I asked, guessing he didn't as we'd walked or taken taxis everywhere since last night.

"No. Do you?" He replied in the same tone. Touché.

"Hardly anyone owns a car in Cardiff," I lied, "you can walk practically everywhere." That part was true.

He quirked an eyebrow at me, "Walking it is then," he left the shop and leaned against my glass window, a clear signal that he was ready to go.

I tilted my head, listening for the tell-tale patter of rain on the glass roof of the Arcade and heard nothing. A walk would be good and probably about as fast as driving in Saturday rush hour traffic, now the shops were shutting. I checked on Errol who was back asleep and grabbed my coat and, after a moment's thought, my axe, before joining Lorandir outside and locking up. The Arcade was practically empty so I wasn't worried about losing business and Aloora was waiting.

Chapter 8

I deliberately didn't tell Lorandir where we were going so I could set the pace rather than racing to keep up with his longer legs. He didn't complain at the slower pace and shortened his stride to match mine as we walked in a silence that somehow felt companionable. We made a quick stop at the Dragon's Head coffee shop so I could grab a mug of coffee laced with chocolate syrup and I bought several brownies as a gift for Aloora. Brinda, the owner, smiled at me as I left, probably thinking they were all for me, but, to her credit, she stayed silent.

The sun was low in the sky as we arrived at Aloora's house, making the Victorian terraced houses look picturesque and romantic with the soft pinkish glow highlighting the brickwork and glinting off the windows. A few pink and orange clouds drifted past on a gentle breeze, and a hint of better weather seemed to be in the air as I stepped onto the tiles outside Aloora's door and knocked.

Aloora opened the door immediately, she must have been waiting for us. I embraced her, nearly crushing her in my relief to see her well.

“Steady on,” she laughed, returning my hug warmly, “and hello you. Thank you for rescuing me.” She looked over my shoulder to Lorandir who gave a stiff half bow as I released my friend and turned. It might have been the dusky light but it seemed as if he was blushing slightly. Great. Another fanboy for Aloora Dragonquest.

She grabbed my hand, squeezed it and led me inside to the kitchen. I was surprised to see Gunther and Marco already seated on one side at the small table, which had a pile of old books stacked in the middle, and greeted them with a smile and commiserations about how tired we all were. I took out my keyring and made to unclip the anti-illusion charm that Gunther had given me to return it to him. He shook his head, pressed his hand over mine and told me to keep it with a serious expression I was unused to seeing.

Aloora made a round of hot drinks and the scent of Marco’s espresso filled the kitchen, competing with Aloora’s herbal tea, creating a strange earthy bitter aroma. After handing out the drinks and setting a large plate of biscuits on the table, Aloora sat daintily on a wobbly chair at the end of the table, and I squeezed onto an uncomfortable metal fold out chair painted in a garish orange, generously leaving Lorandir the remaining wooden seat, also painted orange.

“What’s going on?” I asked as I blew on my milky regular tea, enjoying the warmth of the cup in my hands.

Aloora took a deep breath. “I think we’re in trouble.”

“What?” Marco nearly choked on his espresso.

“The elves that captured me, they were talking about the ritual and I think they have found one of the artefacts and they’re going to do it soon,” Aloora continued, her hands gripped tightly together on the scuffed wooden table.

Judging from the puzzled expressions from everyone around the table, none of us knew what she was talking about. Gunther looked as if he was about to ask if she'd hit her head. I interrupted.

"Sorry Aloora. I have no idea what you're talking about. What ritual? What artefacts? What are they going to do when?"

Aloora sighed and rolled her eyes. "*The* ritual," Seeing our blank expressions, she elaborated. "There's a belief among some dragon scholars that they never left this world, or died out, and rather they slumber beneath the earth waiting to be awakened. There's a legend, a myth, that there is a ritual that will awaken them. No one knows exactly what it is, but there are references to awakenings in some of the dragon texts I've studied," she indicated the pile of books on the table; she'd been recovering by studying dragon rituals. "All of the translations seem clear that some sort of artefact is needed, probably one of the dragon-forged orbs from the golden era, when dragons were allied with, rather than enemies of, the other races, but no one's exactly clear on what it is. I think they have an original scroll with the ritual on it, the elves were arguing about getting me to translate it."

"Why were they arguing?" Gunther leaned forward curiously.

"The male wanted to get me to do it straight away and was talking about forcing me to," Aloora took a breath and gripped her hands more tightly, "the female wanted to talk to me first, trying to sway me to their cause. She did talk to me for a bit. She said she was pleased to meet a fellow dragon lover and admired my translations and work online." Aloora spat the last sentence, clearly unimpressed.

"I am sorry that Espretha kidnapped you," Lorandir spoke softly and raised his green eyes to meet Aloora's blue ones. Aloora nodded.

"Thank you. But it's not your fault. You're not responsible for her."

"If they truly are planning to raise a dragon, we have to stop them," Lorandir replied grimly.

"I agree, I love dragons but I have no wish to meet one," Aloora shuddered although her eyes shined at her favourite topic.

"So the plan is to stop two crazy elves from waking up a dragon and we have no idea what they have found or how much of the ritual they have translated or where they are," I summarised.

"No. The female elf showed me a copy of the scroll they have, she left it in the room with me and I grabbed it while you were talking to the police. I have it here," Aloora pulled a printed piece of paper from her pocket and laid it on the table with a flourish. It was covered in an unfamiliar language I thought was a form of Elvish. "I think there are more of them planning to do something on the Spring Solstice. It makes sense from my studies that it is done on a day of power and magic, any ritual will be more potent on that day. That is one week from today."

We were all silent, realising the implications of the short timeline. Gunther picked up the paper and squinted at it, "Can you translate it?"

"If anyone can, Aloora can," I replied loyally, squeezing Aloora's shoulder.

"I can try," Aloora was modest but her eyes were gleaming at the challenge.

I circled back to something that had been bugging me. "So there are more than two of them who are involved? Any idea how many?"

Aloora shook her head sadly.

Gunther set down the piece of paper and pushed it towards Aloora. "Well I'll help however I can love. Dwarves have legends of dragons and they are not pleasant, we cannot let them return. I'll speak to the Council, they might be able to help. Can you do anything to get the elves to help?"

Lorandir nodded, "I will message our High Council, we too know the dangers of dragons. I cannot believe Espretha would be foolish enough to try to awaken one but we must not allow it happen."

Marco and I glanced at each other, both unsure what we could add to this. Aloora looked to me,

"Can you make anything that would help us just in case?" she asked, reaching out to hold my hand. I was pleased she was involving me.

"I don't think I have anything that could slay a dragon," I mused, "but I can make us something to help even the odds against a group of crazy elves…present company excepted." I glanced at Lorandir, expecting him to be annoyed. Instead he nodded seriously.

"We will need anything you can give us. That male elf was a powerful sorcerer and Espretha is good with blades. If it comes to a fight, your charms will be appreciated."

"But we can stop them before it gets to a fight, no?" Marco chimed in. "They have not translated the ritual. They cannot do it without Aloora, so we keep her safe and they cannot do it."

Aloora made a strange clicking noise with her mouth to disagree with him. "There are others who can translate as well or better than me. But I know someone who can help, Professor Maron. We can go there now."

"Will he be there now? It's Saturday night," Gunther asked.

"He practically lives at the University. He'll be there," she replied confidently.

"I'm going with you," I said, grabbing my coat and a couple of biscuits from the plate on the table.

"And me," Lorandir added, also standing. I didn't feel like arguing and it might be worth having another person who could speak Elvish when we met the eccentric elvish professor.

"I'll contact the Council," Gunther spoke up. He gave us each a dwarfish goodbye by clasping wrists in comradeship before he left.

Marco looked undecided and out of his depth. "I will stay here and cook," he proclaimed. I smiled at him. Marco had inherited his love of cooking from his Italian parents and I was sure there would be a feast by the time we returned from seeing Professor Maron.

Chapter 9

We walked briskly the short distance to the main University building. I walked behind while Aloora and Lorandir talked about internet memes and the latest dragon research she had dug up and shared on her YouTube channel. I was slightly jealous that they were getting along so well. As we crossed the small parking lot where I had been attacked the night before, I glanced anxiously around, surreptitiously checking under the group of cars parked outside the main building. I didn't see any signs of wyrms but I was still tense until we shut the wooden door behind us.

As we signed in, the security guard recognised me from the night before. "Found her then?" he chortled before clocking Lorandir's sword; he was close enough that the invisibility spell wasn't effective. "Er, is that a sword? You can leave it here," he swallowed, his accent sounding much thicker than it had last night. I guessed he was nervous. Mundane people, those without magic, often were in the presence of magical beings and Lorandir was doing nothing to try to hide his elvishness.

Lorandir's hand went to the hilt of his sword and I was expecting an argument when Aloora stepped in front of the elf and brightly told him it was a magic sword and we were taking it to Professor Maron. The guard blinked several times.

“Well I suppose a magic sword isn’t the strangest thing you’ve brought here…I want it recorded though.”

Aloora nodded cheerfully and wrote “magic sword” next to Lorandir’s name on the sign in book in neat cursive. She ushered us quickly along the worn red carpet and upstairs to find the Professor’s office.

“What was that about?” I asked when we were out of earshot.

“What?” Aloora blinked innocently as if being accused of bringing strange things into the University was entirely normal. I narrowed my eyes at my friend. “We’re here.”

She stopped by an aged wooden door with a brass handle and key hole that would have looked more at home in a stately manor. A brass nameplate next to the door proclaimed it belonged to Professor E Maron. The weirdest thing about the door was a large cast iron door knocker shaped like a dragon eating its own tail just below a peephole carved into the door.

Unphased, Aloora knocked three times on the Professor’s door knocker then flung it open. The elf sitting at the desk looked old, with white hair and a long thin moustache drooping past his chin. He was wearing quintessential professor clothing of a green tweed jacket with leather elbow patches over jeans and I wondered if there was a special shop for academics.

“Ah, the lovely Dragonquest. How goes the questing?” He smiled at Aloora then noticed Lorandir and I lurking behind her petite frame. “And some fellow adventurers I see, welcome, welcome to my realm.”

I stepped into the room, which was lined with bookcases. Compared to the filing system in here, Aloora’s ransacked room looked neat.

There were piles of books and scrolls everywhere, pouring out from the shelves and stacked on the floor. More piles of paper had fallen from his desk in an avalanche that I had the impression had been there for a while as some of the papers had a distinctly yellowed look.

"Hi Elrond, we could use your help with a new scroll…"

The Professor steepled his fingers and regarded us with interest but replied noncommittally, "Hmmm."

"Of course if you're too busy…" Aloora started to turn as if to leave the room.

His eyes twinkled. "Never too busy for you my dear! But we must observe protocols! Tea! Then to business." He plugged an electric kettle into a socket right below a yellow warning sign saying *for laptops and phone chargers only. Danger do not use for other appliances*, and started to spoon tea leaves into an antique teapot.

Aloora caught my eye and winked. "Elrond?" I mouthed. She shrugged. The Professor must have seen me though because he chuckled.

"Yes Elrond. It's a common enough elvish name. It is a blessing and a curse. I knew him you see, Ronald Tolkien, we taught at Oxford together and bonded over languages. I was obsessed with ancient Draconian while he was interested in Elvish as well as Anglo-Saxon. It is to my great pride and regret that he used the name in his magnum opus, for no one ever believes it is my real name. I assure you however, that I came before Lord of the Rings!" He finished with a flourish and a small bow, making his moustache droop dangerously close to the hot water which he was now pouring into the pot.

As we waited for the tea to brew, my eyes wandered along the spines of books I could see, I wasn't surprised that I couldn't understand many of them but the ones in English were all about dragons: *Dragons and their beginnings, Dragons and the dinosaurs, Dragons: Myth and Fact* and even a dog eared copy of *The Dragon Book of Jokes*. I paused in my perusal of the shelves to take the tea cup the Professor thrust into my hands and blew on it as he gestured for me to take a seat on a chair vacated from its stack of books after he had plonked them on the floor right next to it.

"So, a gnome, an elf and a dwarf walk into my office…it's either a joke or the start of a fantasy novel," he smiled to himself.

"Half-dwarf," I muttered to myself.

"Of course, but that doesn't fit my joke!" Curse his elvish hearing. "So the question is, why are you here? You need my help with your quest, obviously, so you have found something that even the delectable Ms Dragonquest cannot translate. So what is it about dragons that you have found?"

I forced myself to keep still. He had told us exactly what Aloora had told him in about three times as many words.

Aloora leant forward. "I think it's about the awakening ritual. These runes fit with other texts I've seen and been posting about recently, but there's a lot here that's new to me and Draconic is a contextual language," I was sure she added the last part for mine and Lorandir's benefit. The old elf leant forward and studied the print out that Aloora laid onto his desk, familiarly clearing some space by brushing papers to one side. He either didn't notice or didn't care that this pushed a couple of other pieces of paper onto the avalanche by his desk.

He took a pair of pince-nez spectacles from a pocket and balanced them on his hooked nose. He inhaled sharply, "Well, well, well, my dear, this is a find indeed. Where did you get this from?" His blue eyes were sharp as they rested on Aloora.

She met his gaze calmly. “I think someone’s trying to perform it. They want to raise a dragon.” He shifted his gaze to Lorandir then me, we nodded mutely.

“Then they are fools,” Elrond declared. Again we nodded, “but it is not as easy as reading words on paper. This is a *ritual*.”

“Sorry but what does that mean?” I sounded stupid, this was a world away from running a shop.

“It means, my dear half-dwarf, that one must be in the right place at the right time with the right equipment and the right words.”

“And is that time the Summer Solstice?” I thought back to Aloora’s grim prediction from earlier.

His eyes pierced me. “Ye-es, it could be,” he bent back over the paper and then poked at it “Here, it says here it must be a day of power. So, theoretically, it could be a solstice or a midwinter or midsummer, then of course there are other days of power, equinoxes for example.” He spun in his chair, the leather creaking slightly as he dug through a stack of papers.

“Hah!” he exclaimed triumphantly, waving a pad of paper in the air. He threw it at me. I caught it but spilled my tea onto the floor. I carefully placed my cup down before rearranging the pad so I could read it. It was a calendar, from six years ago. As I flicked through, I noticed that the dates were falling on the same day and that days of power were marked with red text. I gulped. There were a lot more dates than I expected. I flicked back to March, but only the equinox or Spring Solstice in March was highlighted, so they could do it next week or they’d have to wait until, I turned the page, April 1st.

“April Fool’s Day is a day of power?” I couldn’t stop myself.

The Professor laughed heartily, “Why of course. What better day to do something foolish than a day for fools? And trying to raise a dragon is foolish! But if you truly do have people trying to do this,

I suspect the Spring Solstice is a more romantic date… Now dates aside, what does one need to perform a ritual?"

"An artefact?" Lorandir volunteered.

"Yes, yes my boy, but what type? Will any old magic doodad do?" He moved his finger along the page. "No, this is specific. You need a very specific artefact for this to work, something imbued with dragon magic and something of a dragon. If I'm reading it right, that means a piece of a dragon. That is very difficult to get hold of."

"What about fossils?" I interrupted.

"A good question! But, this means a literal piece of a dragon; dragon flesh or blood or claw or tooth or scale, not fossilised rock. If they think it will work with a fossilised claw then you have nothing to worry about. And then there are the words, which must be imbued with powerful magic, an ordinary person will not have the force to conjure them into power that would raise a dragon," to illustrate his point, he read the text, his voice guttural in the pronunciation of the ancient language. I held my breath. Nothing happened. I breathed out again.

The Professor laughed, "You see. Now I don't know what all these words mean, that one is 'awaken', that one is I think 'rise'. And of course I need to know so I can intend the meaning of the ritual. That is important! Without intent or power, the words are next to meaningless. And typically Draconic rituals require an offering as well…blood or flesh usually I'm afraid. I will need to take a copy to work on a full translation."

Aloora looked at us then nodded to the Professor who laughed with glee and rushed out of the room to the photocopier down the hall.

"He's nuts," I whispered to Aloora.

"He's brilliant," she sounded hurt. He was probably the equivalent of a rock star to her. I squeezed her hand as an apology and mouthed, "Sorry."

The Professor returned in a whirlwind of energy. "A copy for you and a copy for me. I shall call you when I have something."

"You mentioned the right place?" Lorandir's voice sounded muffled in the office.

"Quite right. I did. None of this will work unless you know where a sleeping dragon lies!" The Professor strode across the room and rocked on the soles of his feet a few times before he began pulling books out of a bookshelf. "These are theories on where dragons might be sleeping. Some are hogwash, after all fault lines are clearly responsible for some earthquakes and not even a snoring dragon could get above a five on the Richter scale. Browne has some interesting ideas, as does Petrovsky and Melathir, his work is in Elvish, but you won't have any trouble with that. I never did go for dragon location studies so you can borrow these while I translate." He shoved a stack of books onto Lorandir.

"Thank you," the younger elf was solemn.

As we got up to leave, Aloora asked softly, "Is it possible?"

The Professor met our eyes one by one, "Oh yes, I'm afraid it is. Improbable of course. But if these people you are so worried about have found the words then they may well have the other parts or a means to get them. You must tread carefully; anyone who seriously considers raising a dragon is someone who is dangerous."

We nodded. Schiztz. This was serious. Professor Maron bowed us out of the door and I thought I spotted a camp bed covered in books behind the door as we left, maybe he really did live at the University.

"Who keeps a calendar from 6 years ago?" I mumbled to myself as we left.

"The days always come round again young half-dwarf! Until next time!" Bloody elvish hearing.

We divvied up the sizeable pile of books that Lorandir had staggered downstairs with, waved to the security guard on the way out and walked back to Aloora's in silence. I relaxed once we had made it out of the University gates, the wyrm attack still making me watchful. It seemed unthinkable that someone or a group of someones were trying to raise a dragon, yet Aloora had been kidnapped and the Professor had believed us. We entered the house in a sombre mood but I instantly perked up when the delicious aroma of cooking greeted us.

Marco was amazing, he had cooked a rich tagliatelle carbonara and whipped up garlic bread to accompany it. I almost raced to the kitchen and sat down hungrily watching as Marco dished up the creamy pasta.

I gulped down several mouthfuls while the others took their seats. "This is a-ma-zing."

"Thank you, thank you," Marco fluttered his hands in a self-deprecating manner. "It was nothing, but I think you have news, yes?"

I let Aloora fill him in while I focused on eating and drinking the heady red wine Marco had poured. It was smooth and warming and I was very grateful for the normality of eating with friends after the last two days. After my second portion of carbonara, I used the last of the crusty garlic bread to mop up any last smidgen of sauce from the standard plain white student-starter set plate.

"So, we think we know the date and the crazy elves have the words, no offense…" he waved at Lorandir who nodded. "…but they don't know what they mean so they cannot intend the ritual right. But in case they do translate them, we should find the location and this artefact." Marco rubbed his hands together. "Where do we start?"

Aloora squinted her eyes, "I should focus on translating, if I can help Professor Maron it will speed things up. Draconian runes often have different meanings and…" She trailed off, aware our eyes had glazed over, "you can work on the location so we have something to share with the Dwarven and Elvish High Councils."

Lorandir pushed back his chair as he left the room with his phone out to contact the Elvish High Council. I checked my phone, no word from Gunther. Aloora vanished into her room to focus on the print out and Marco and I stared at each other before shrugging and clearing the table.

We split the pile of books into two, ignoring the one in Elvish and began flicking through them. Marco held up a centrefold from the largest book and showed it to me. "This is the world! They could be anywhere!"

I rubbed my eyes, "Well, they're in the UK so let's narrow it down to that location. There are enough legends of dragons here that it makes sense there will be locations here, and Wales is the land of the dragons after all. There's even one on the flag!" That made sense to me, but was it right? It was feasible that the elves and their gang could hop on a flight to anywhere in the next week but they had a flat here in Cardiff and why wouldn't they go elsewhere to get their ritual translated? They were keeping local for a reason I guessed.

Marco nodded then slammed the book down and raced upstairs. I turned back to my book, which despite being billed as a *Quest for Dragons*, was an incredibly dull account of the author's travels around Europe. I heard Marco's steps returning and looked up expectantly. He was carrying an A0 size poster of the UK and a lot of pins.

“It was a gift when I moved here,” he explained as he attached it to the cork notice board on the wall of the kitchen. It overhung by a lot so we pinned it into the wall as well. I hoped the pin sized holes wouldn’t affect their student deposits but I knew how picky landlords could be. As we were attaching the map to the wall, I heard a raised voice in the hall before Lorandir marched in.

“They don’t believe me,” he said incredulously, glaring at his phone before throwing it on the table. “Two of our own kind, maybe more, ignoring all warnings and trying to wake a dragon, and those bloody idiots won’t do more than try to contact Espretha!” Lorandir was exasperated and it was the first time I’d seen him express so much emotion.

Smothering the British instinct to offer him a cup of tea, I shoved the Elvish book that the Professor had given us towards him. “We’d better try to find the location then, so we can get it watched,” I had no idea how we were going to do that, but the Dwarves might be more amenable to helping.

As we read, we pinned any UK location that the authors had marked as a potential for a location for a sleeping dragon. There were some general consistencies around them needing a lot of space, peace and quiet and likely to be underground, but there were a lot of discrepancies between the experts who wrote the books. Browne focused on hills and cave networks whereas Petrovsky was more concerned with fairy circles and places of power. This led to a lot of seemingly random pins placed into the map.

After three hours of speed reading and many cups of tea, I had had enough. I blinked at the map trying to focus when something occurred to me. There were a small number of locations that had several pins in them and two were near Cardiff, with lots more single pins dotted around the city as well.

"Guys, I think we should focus on Cardiff…" Lorandir and Marco looked up and I indicated the pins. "There could be a dragon under us!" The thought was uncomfortable but my gut told me I was onto something, why else were the elves here? Marco grabbed a load of post-its and handed them out. Any time Cardiff or a nearby location was mentioned, we placed a post-it in the book and I dropped a pin into the map app on my phone. An uncomfortable pattern emerged.

I held up my phone. "It looks like there could be a dragon under Cardiff Castle…"

Marco swore softly in Italian while Lorandir furrowed his smooth forehead. "Are there any other places with as many pins?"

I zoomed the map out so it covered most of South Wales. "Actually, yes," I surprised myself and zoomed in on another location nearby, "it's another castle, Castell Coch."

I supressed a snort of laughter, I'd lived in Cardiff long enough to have heard the castle's name many times but Coch, pronounced roughly as cock by those who tried their best and meaning "red" in Welsh, still sounded funny to me.

"Did Espretha mention anything about either castle?" I asked.

Lorandir shook his head. I shouted for Aloora to come in. She almost ran in then stopped when she saw our map and faces.

I cut to the chase. "The dragon might be under Cardiff Castle or Castell Coch."

She considered then shrugged. "There's a theory that certain monuments might be designed to protect dragons or prevent them from waking. Castles would fit that. And it makes sense it would be in Cardiff, else why wouldn't the elves take me somewhere else or pick someone else, I'm not the only person proficient in Draconian."

We all stared at her, she knew that all along! "You are the only person who regularly broadcasts their location on social media though," I felt I had to claw back some of our triumph at finding two likely locations.

Aloora nodded, "I don't think we can do much more tonight, I'll text the Professor with what we've found and my progress on the translation and we can meet up tomorrow."

Lorandir shifted uncomfortably, "Actually, I was hoping to stay with Espretha, but…"

"Where did you stay yesterday?" Aloora asked curiously.

Lorandir looked at me, "With Amethyst…" Aloora shot me a curious look.

I folded my arms. "It was….well there's no room really," Great. That made it sound more suspicious.

Marco offered up the sofa in their shared house and we said our goodbyes after I turned down Lorandir's offer to walk me home. I wanted to walk alone in the fresh night air to clear my head from the wine I had been drinking and the discovery that we could be walking on top of a dragon.

I decided to walk past the museum and Town Hall to get home rather than follow the road to the main pedestrianised area. It also took me past Cardiff Castle and I had a strange desire to see the building and reassure myself it was a castle, not a dragon's resting place. The best I could do was look at walls and the keep that peeked over the high walls. I walked quickly, staying alert for rogue wyrms, my hand on Bane.

As I walked past the museum, I looked up at the flags swaying in the light breeze which displayed the show piece of the current exhibit. It looked like a large claw or tooth mounted into a golden hilt that had a single emerald placed into its front. I read the name of the exhibition spelled out in both English and Welsh and then the smaller text about the dagger with a sinking feeling.

Dragons - The Exhibition – Dragon-forged Fang Dagger.

I took a picture on my smartphone and sent to Aloora. She immediately texted back. *I'm on my way.*

This was bad; an artefact that could be used in the ritual was being stored here in Cardiff in the National Museum. I walked closer, heading up the steps to the imposing stone columns that fronted the museum. There was no one around that I could sense. I tried the heavy wooden doors at the front entrance. They were locked and judging by their size, the only way someone could break in was with a small battering ram. Good. My phone buzzed. Another text from Aloora.

Meet me at the Professor's office.

Now I had no idea what was going on, but I jogged the few minutes back from the museum to the main University building practically next door, signed in again as the security guard joked that I couldn't stay away and ran upstairs to his office. I couldn't remember exactly where it was along the corridor so I slowed down to read the name plates until I found his office. Low murmuring from inside suggested Aloora was already there. I knocked then pushed the door open.

Aloora was indeed sat down in Professor Maron's office, as were both Lorandir and Marco. The Professor was standing by his kettle, in the process of making tea.

The Professor clapped his hands together gleefully as I entered. "Well, well, well. The group of adventurers has found an artefact, and so soon! It could of course be coincidence…but it is entirely possible that this could be used in the ritual, especially because I have made progress with the translation. It seems that blood must be spilled to awaken a dragon, they are predators after all. This dagger could do that." Aloora nodded, confirming his grim assessment of the translation. The Professor handed out well-brewed cups of herbal tea to all of us.

"We need to warn somebody," Lorandir stood as if he would march out of the room right now.

The Professor gestured dismissively, "Yes, yes. I'm good friends with the curator of the exhibit, I was planning to go myself actually. It's rare to see so many pieces of dragon history together, ironically to celebrate the Spring Solstice, rebirth and all that. The dagger is to be the showpiece…." He seemed to realise he was rambling. "Anyway, I've called her and the dagger is so valuable they aren't putting it on display until the start of the exhibition. It's locked up at the owner's vault until then and will be travelling under top security."

I thought back to the dates on the flag. "The exhibition starts on Monday!"

"Exactly, my young half-dwarf. So, Mei, that's the curator, will meet us tomorrow afternoon and we can tell her all about our fears. We can stop this particular artefact from getting into their hands. We must hope this is what they are after," he gazed into middle distance for a time before rubbing his hands together, "now, it is the witching hour. I suggest you all return to your beds and get some rest. I will see you in the museum lobby at four p.m. sharp."

I was about to apologise for disturbing him, but the old elf seemed excited and Aloora had been the one to contact him, so with a smile from the Professor and worried glances between the rest of us, we left the messy office and exited the building. I felt a pang of loneliness as the other three went back to Aloora and Marco's house share but squashed it down and kept my goodbyes light and breezy before walking very quickly home. This time, I chose the slightly longer route through the main pedestrianised centre, I wanted bright lights and people around, even if it was drunken students on their way between clubs. I had never been gladder to see Errol than when I rushed into my shop cum home and let him curl up in bed with me that night, a welcome hot water bottle soothing the anxious thoughts that were whirling around my head.

Chapter 10

I awoke early. My dreams had been confused visions of massive dragons trying to eat Aloora and fire surrounding me. I shook my head as if that would get rid of the uneasiness I felt. Errol grumbled as I pushed him aside to get some cereal. I had forgotten to get milk with all the excitement yesterday, so made do with toast and some out of date jam. I figured it had so much sugar in it, it was bound to be OK.

I took a long shower in peace before shoving on an oversized iron man t-shirt and black jeans and heading down to the forge. The Royal Arcade didn't open until eleven a.m. on Sundays so I had some time to myself before I would open the shop. I gave Errol a bucket of coal and refilled his water bowl as I contemplated my tools and materials. I wanted to make something that would help us, but what could help against dragons…if it came to the worst.

I chewed my lip as I thought, and eventually decided that protection from fire would be useful. With Errol's help I forged five flame-shaped golden charms, imbued with magic to stop the wearer being burned. I had given them a cartoonish shape and they looked quite sweet, so I made an extra couple to sell in the shop, glad that my dwarven heritage meant I was a quick crafter. I strung my charm onto my key chain alongside the anti-elvish glamour charm that Gunther had given me and decided to test it. I gave Errol the command for "Fire" and pointed to my shoe. Errol was well trained but he gave me a look and didn't spout any flames until I gave the command a second time. Then he blasted out a spurt of fire that flickered on my boot. It felt warm, but not unpleasantly so and I was pleased to see that the rubber sole on my leather boot was undamaged. The charms worked. Errol snorted and I rewarded him with a piece of charcoal and a scratch behind his ear before he curled up and went back to sleep.

It was with a self-satisfied smile that I opened up my shop that day. It was slow trading compared to Saturday but I still managed to sell a few pieces of jewellery including one of my new fire charms. The hours passed slowly, but finally it was time to close up and get to the museum.

I arrived at the same time a number of tourists were leaving but the steps outside were so wide, I avoided them easily and stepped inside. I scanned the lobby. It was surprisingly light for such a large building. Pale coloured columns drew the eye upwards to the light open galleries upstairs. My eyes alighted on the huge black dragon skeleton arranged as if it were about to take off. I gaped, it was larger than Dippy the Diplodocus who had been doing a tour of the UK and I thought had filled the space when I had seen it in the museum last year. Next to the ominous skeleton, I spotted the Professor talking to a small Chinese lady with a neat black bob and a fitted jacket over tight jeans. I wandered over and in a broad Scottish accent, she introduced herself as Mei, the curator of the new exhibit. She smiled as we shook hands, and then we waited awkwardly for the others.

Fortunately, they arrived soon after and interrupted the start of what looked like becoming a discourse on the intricacies of historic elvish politics as the Professor began to fill the awkward silence.

After introductions, Mei cut to the chase. "Elrond tells me you're interested in my new exhibition. I'm really excited about it, let me show you around." She waved away the member of staff who had been heading in our direction to ensure we knew it was almost closing time and led us briskly past the gift shop into the Evolution of Wales gallery.

"We've completely reorganised this gallery so all the dragon fossils found in Wales are together and the British Museum has loaned us the complete skeleton you saw in the lobby. This is the first time so many dragon related pieces have been together at any museum," she noticed we were all staring upwards at the massive skull suspended from the ceiling and smiled like a fond mother, "We call her the Meglodragon. Or Meg for short. She's the largest known dragon skull ever found and she was found not too far from here, in Llantwit Major."

"She?" interrupted Lorandir.

"Oh yes, dragons were matriarchal, the largest were always female. They also had the venom – look closely, can you see the arc in the top jaw there? Well that's where the muscles attached to the venom sac would have connected. Males don't have them. Now after this, you can see a bit of dragon and other species interaction through the ages as we carry on this way." Mei led us around the gallery, commenting on various dioramas and other finds throughout the Evolution of Wales. We ended up back in the lobby and Mei gave a bright smile as she followed large red dragon footprints stuck to the floor to a smaller gallery.

"In here are the crown jewels so to speak. I've been persuading private collectors to loan us their dragon objects for years."

"Don't museums have the right to first bid on dragon artefacts?" I asked, recalling something I'd read in the paper a few years back when a large hoard of treasure had been discovered in a field.

"Well yes and no. If the item was found post 1996 then yes, but before that it went to the highest bidder and dragon forged items are not only rare, they are extremely valuable. We've got the dragon blade from a family that has had it handed down through generations. It's been a real coup to get all of these together," she gestured to the gallery and we all split up to look at the pieces.

One side was titled *Inspiration from Dragons* and included modern art sculptures, clothing from a famous fashion designer and older renaissance artworks that looked vaguely familiar. The other side held dragon related items. I paused in front of a football sized fossilised dragon's egg with a blue tinge to it that had been mounted in a silver egg cup covered with sapphires. No wonder Mei was pleased with her exhibition, I thought, as I read the plaque noting it was on loan from a private collection. I contemplated the weapons that claimed to have slain dragons that lined the wall. There was a mix of swords, including one shaped like a scimitar and even an axe. I wondered if that might be the real Bane of legend but there was nothing on the small plaque next to it.

The blades all still looked sharp from what I could tell, indicating dwarven craftsmanship, and I was giving them a critical eye when I noticed Lorandir next to me.

He smiled, "Almost as good as the one you made for me."

I bristled, as much on principle as anything else, but I could be in real trouble with the Dwarven Arms Council if they thought I was advertising my goods as dwarven. "My skill is nothing like what would be required to make a blade capable of killing a dragon. See how the metal glints on all of them and the blades are still sharp, that's blue forged steel, a secret only known to master dwarf smiths. It can take a hundred years to produce. I can feel the enchantments on some of them from here, these are powerful blades. My weapons can put down more mundane threats but not a dragon!" I realised my voice had risen and I had said too much as I felt everyone else's eyes on me.

The Professor coughed. "Well, that's all well and good my fair half-dwarf, but it seems to me that there is one glaring omission in this exhibit," he waved towards an empty podium in the centre of the room.

Mei smiled again. "Yes, the Fang Dagger. This is the only known example of a dragon-forged blade in the UK. It's unique and very valuable, not just because of the jewels in its hilt. Legend has it that it was an incisor from the famous emerald dragon Baskelique herself. She gifted it to the elf king Lunaster to thank him for fighting alongside the dragon against the Mostrim in the battle of Babylon. She worked with the elvish smiths to forge the ceremonial Fang Dagger to commemorate the alliance and bring peace with the elves. Of course, that was when dragons and other races still co-existed with relative harmony, the Mostrim aside. That race seems to have fought everyone, which is probably why they were hunted down all those thousands of years ago."

"You said ceremonial?" I interrupted what was building into a discourse on ancient history.

Mei's look turned thoughtful. "Yes, but it was still used as a weapon. Lunaster allegedly used it as his second favourite weapon after his sword, Novestri. That is said to be an exquisite sword but the elves guard it preciously, I haven't even been able to see it," she finished wistfully, looking at Lorandir, who looked away.

The Professor picked up the conversation. “The Fang Dagger is indeed an important exhibit, and its history is illustrious, but why isn’t it here?”

Mei shrugged, “The collector was very particular about security, it’s arriving at nine a.m. tomorrow morning with an armed security escort. They are also providing two additional security guards to man the exhibit at all times and of course our museum security has been upped as well. That’s a pressure release pad on the podium that will trigger an alarm and a lockdown if it is released, and of course we’ll have bullet proof glass around it once it’s in place. It’s a real rarity that it’s on display at all, this is the first time it will be in public for nearly a hundred years, so I’m happy to accommodate the extra security. You’ll come and see it tomorrow I hope,” she smiled round us and then faltered at our grim expressions.

The Professor stepped forward. “Well, Mei…actually we were rather hoping you might not show it.” The small lady spluttered and he spoke again quickly, “You see we have reason to believe that there are people who want to use it to try to awaken a dragon.”

“Impossible!” She snorted.

Aloora spoke softly. “I was kidnapped by two elves who thought they could do it, they have a ritual and…”

“The fact that you were kidnapped by elves does not change my exhibition. I have been planning this for two years, trekking the country, agreeing to insane demands to get it to happen. No ritual has ever been found for waking a dragon, if they even do still slumber and aren’t all dead. The power it would take…and you don’t even know for sure that they want this dagger do you?” Mei squinted at us dangerously.

We couldn’t deny it but the Professor kept trying. “If there is even the slightest risk to the dagger, surely your patron should be informed. Let me talk to them and they can decide on the best course of action."

"Absolutely not! I expected better of you Elrond than chasing after dragons at your age. The exhibition will go ahead as planned. That is my final word on the matter. Now if you'll excuse me, I have some last minute details to attend to." Mei stormed off.

"Well that went well," I couldn't help myself.

The Professor didn't look disheartened though. "We shall just have to be here ourselves to help. We know what we're looking for – people, probably elves, who are too interested in the dagger, and there's nothing to stop me speaking to the security guards tomorrow, they may well pass on our concerns to this patron."

Aloora invited the Professor and I back to her house to plan and Marco ordered pizza for us all. Aloora had sighed and plumped for a salad. That gnome was so healthy it was sickening. I pulled a slice of four cheese pizza from the box and waved it. "How do we know it will happen tomorrow?"

The Professor closed his eyes for a moment. "We don't know for sure of course," he admitted before going on quickly, "the easiest time to attempt a heist would be towards the end of the exhibition when security is more comfortable, I expect. But our elves need to be in possession of the artefact before Saturday if they are attempting the ritual on the Solstice and I'm sure there are other things to prepare, so they will want it well ahead of Saturday. And why not sooner than later? Better to have it in hand on day one than risk anyone getting wind of their plans, especially since Aloora escaped. I would think the easiest time to get it will be at the beginning of the exhibition, when it's being moved."

Professor Maron was persuasive but it was all supposition. I stayed quiet and ate my pizza while the others planned. The basic plan was to get into the exhibit and stay there all day, watching for any suspicious activity and trying not to act suspiciously ourselves. The Professor would put security on alert and try other channels to get the Fang Dagger safely back in its vault until after the Solstice. I handed out protection charms and the fire charms I had made that morning.

Marco pouted, “I wanted jewellery not key rings.”

“Jewellery costs extra,” I smiled, making a mental note to make him something for his birthday. As I handed one to Lorandir, my mind wandered to our first meeting and his invisible sword. “What about invisibility?” I blurted out. The others stared at me.

“You have a way to be invisible?” Marco asked, eyes wide in astonishment.

“Um, well no. But he does,” I pointed at Lorandir.

The elf narrowed his eyes, “I can cast an enchantment on an object so it is not visible from a distance, but I can’t make people invisible.” He thought a moment, “I could make you all less noticeable though, we would blend into the background more.”

Aloora nodded, “Sounds good. You can cast that on us tomorrow. So the plan is to meet at the park opposite the museum, eight thirty a.m. sharp.”

As I nodded in agreement, my phone rang. I saw Gunther’s contact info flash up and answered the call.

“Amethyst, my treasure, how are you?” I filled him in on our plan tomorrow and asked how it had gone with the Council. His voice hardened, “They didn’t believe anyone could waken a dragon. When I told them about Aloora’s kidnapping, they said it was an elvish matter. They don’t even believe there are any of the creatures sleeping. They said dwarfs tunnel deeper than anyone and they’d know if there were still dragons. They wouldn’t know a dragon if it bit them on the arse! Bunch of self-important short-sighted selfish dung rats."

I was taken aback, for a full-blooded dwarf to insult the Dwarven Arms Council was unheard of. I raised my head from the phone to see everyone pretending not to listen in.

"The dwarves aren't going to help," I summarised. There were murmurs of disappointment from the others, but no one was too surprised.

I put the phone back to my ear, "I understand if you don't want to get involved."

Gunther snorted, "Blow that! I'll be there tomorrow." He hung up.

"Gunther's in," I informed the rest of the group.

"Wonderful! A full house. And now I must get back to the museum, the sooner I can translate the ritual, the sooner we will have more clues to help us stop this awakening." I offered to walk the Professor back to the main University building and, after exchanging notes with Aloora on the translation so far, we left.

The walk back was illuminated by street lights and some stars twinkled dimly in the dark sky. It felt a lot later than it actually was and the traffic was quiet as it was Sunday evening, casting a strange eerie feel to the city until a police car raced by with blue lights flashing and a siren blaring.

The Professor walked slowly, seeming to delight in the night air and being out of his office, and what I secretly thought might be his bedroom too. As we ambled back to the University, he pointed out landmarks in the distance and gave me a history of the city. He was an engaging conversationalist and the time passed quickly despite our slow pace.

At the University gates, we paused.

"Do you really think we can stop them?" I asked him quietly. It was surprising how quickly I had gone from disbelief that dragons really slept underneath us to believing whole heartedly that a cult was planning on waking one of the creatures right here in Cardiff and I was helping to stop them.

The orange street lights seemed to make his eyes glow slightly as he met my gaze and gripped one of my hands between his own. His skin felt like cool paper to touch. "Young adventurer, these are troubling times, but I have lived a long time and it seems to me as if all times are troubled. And often, it is not the work of governments or politicians that change the times, but the deeds of a small group of determined people. We may hope we are wrong and there is no conspiracy to awaken dragons, but if there is, we will be prepared. We may be small in number but we are significant and we will do our best."

"Thank you," We said farewell and I watched him carefully as he walked across the small lawn and the empty car park, looking up at the sky before disappearing into the main entrance. I released the breath I wasn't aware I had been holding and shivered, I was clearly still affected by the wyrm attack here. I hugged my arms and glanced around. It was quiet. Get it together Amethyst! I forced myself to walk, but as I passed the museum again with its flags streaming in the breeze, I shuddered and sped up.

Chapter 11

I awoke from another night of restless sleep, despite forcing Errol to go for a walk along the brightly lit main shopping streets before it got too late. Trying to tire myself out hadn't worked and I bought myself a bag of jelly sweets as I walked back to the museum. I had a feeling I would need sugar to try to stay alert.

We met, as planned, in the park opposite the museum and watched the entrance. The museum didn't open until ten a.m. and there was plenty of time before the delivery of the Fang Dagger. I had picked us up some hot drinks from the Dragon's Head on the way in cardboard takeaway cups and I held mine, enjoying the warmth seeping into my hands and the sweet aroma of hot chocolate.

After the initial greetings, Lorandir offered to cast an enchantment on us so we'd be less noticeable. He closed his eyes and flicked his fingers at each of us in turn. When it was my turn, I felt the golden honey flavour of his magic tingle down me, and had the comforting warming sensation of drinking sweet mead and eating dark chocolate whilst somehow also feeling as if I was in a sunlit wood. I gasped involuntarily, Lorandir had a lot of power and I felt the glow of his magic as the enchantment settled on me.

“I’ve made your axe invisible at distance, the same as the sword you made me,” I stared at it stupidly. I pulled my goggles down over my eyes and noticed a golden shimmer over the usual dwarfish magic that surrounded my axe.

“Thank you,” sometimes I was very articulate!

After the initial excitement of being enchanted, a grim mood took hold and we watched in silence, sipping the hot drinks.

There were a few parked cars between us and the museum but it was quiet here compared to the busy street running adjacent to us, filled with Monday morning commuter traffic.

A black van pulled up, disregarding the double yellow lines. I tensed and felt the others do the same. A pair of burly guards in black suits got out of the front and walked round to the back to open the van doors. They looked our way but decided we were not a threat, possibly due to Lorandir’s enchantment, and pulled the doors open. Another two guards stepped out and one of them leant back in and pulled out a metal suitcase. It looked like it had a state of the art locking system on it. This had to be the Fang Dagger.

A slight figure approached them from behind a column. We all started forward, before the Professor recognised Mei and whispered to us to hold our positions. He was the only one enjoying acting like we were in some sort of special ops team. He motioned to us to turn around so Mei wouldn’t recognise us and chase us away. It worked. Mei accompanied the guards inside. A jogger ran past and a few people in suits and uniforms with sensible trainers walked through the park on their way to work. So far, so good, no suspicious activity.

As soon as the museum opened, we entered in two groups of three to try to avoid suspicion. Lorandir and I trying to stay back so our weapons were less visible whilst Gunther declared his axe was a cultural piece. When he started to make a fuss, Lorandir and I darted in and tried to stay nonchalant. The museum security decided they weren't paid to deal with Gunther's cultural arguments and, taking in his fitted embroidered waistcoat and tailored trousers, told him to keep it sheathed. They watched him go, muttering about "bloody dwarves" as they glared after him.

We were in! We split up as per the plan. We would take it in shifts with three of us in the main exhibition room and the other three loitering around the rest of the museum, looking for anything suspicious. Aloora, Professor Maron and Gunther went to the exhibition room first.

I heard the Professor starting to tell the security guards about our suspicions when Mei rushed past, heading towards him with intent. We would be lucky not to be thrown out at this rate.

Marco, Lorandir and I split up and wandered around the museum trying to find a good vantage point to watch the lobby and remain unobtrusive. I quickly got too hot, but didn't want to risk drawing attention to my axe by removing my coat, even if the weapon was enchanted.

The day passed slowly. I had wandered around most of the museum several times and had sampled a lot of the café's treats as well as finishing the colourful jelly sweets I had brought with me. I was bored and had taken to looking at the paintings and other items on display with my goggles on to see which ones were enchanted.

I was surprised that some of the more famous paintings had a glimmer of glamour on them, probably what made them attractive. One strange square jade vase glowed with slimy green goblin magic and I had a feeling there was more to it than it seemed.

It was nearly closing time and nothing had happened. I was kicking my heels in the lobby when I heard a snippet of a conversation.

"I still don't understand why it's sunset," a female voice complained, "the sooner, the better."

"The day will have time to build up more power, sunset is the most powerful time on the Solstice. He explained that, weren't you listening? This is our chance to redeem ourselves. Be grateful."

That didn't sound good. I looked up quickly. Two tall figures in oversized hoodies were strolling across the lobby. Their grey hoods were pulled over their heads. Instantly suspicious, I pulled my enchanting goggles down over my eyes and confirmed the forest green aura of two full-blooded elves. They seemed familiar and my heart sank. I grabbed my phone and sent a group message to everyone:

Be alert. 2 elves on way to exhibit

Then I fell into step behind them. The enchantment that Lorandir had placed on me seemed to be working because they didn't so much as turn around as I followed them into the exhibition room.

There were two other people in the room perusing the exhibits. Two security guards stood menacingly by the entrance, dark sunglasses and black suits making them seem like every intimidating security guard in the films. A museum employee in a creased shirt sat on a plastic chair eyeing the clock. Aloora was in the back corner, almost hidden as she sat right next to a stand holding a large ancient book, opened onto a page of St George slaying a fearsome dragon. The Professor was standing next to the weapons, looking absorbed. I almost didn't see Gunther, but I had kept my goggles on and his dark red aura was in the other back corner. I nodded to the two hooded figures and we all began to casually move closer.

Lorandir and Marco shuffled in, just as the two elves reached the Fang Dagger's podium. They had ignored the rest of the exhibition and were staring at the Dagger, which glowed a fierce gold colour under my goggle's gaze. As we started to move to surround them, the smaller of the two, the one I thought was female, pulled something round out of her hoodie pocket. I had a very bad feeling about this. She dropped it casually to the ground. There was a blinding flash of light followed by billowing smoke.

One of the security guards immediately spoke into his microphone while the other one shouted "Stop!" Both moved forward quickly but the purplish smoke made it hard to see. There were confused shouts from the museum employee and the two tourists. The fire alarm started beeping, adding to the cacophony of noise. Then the sprinkler system activated. It was chaos.

With my goggles, I was able to see more than most. The two elves with the forest green auras were leaning over the podium. The Dagger continued to glow like molten gold. I rushed forward, raising Bane, and I heard the smash of glass and a new alarm began to blare.

I stopped as suddenly as if I had run into a wall. I could move a little, but it was like pushing through thick toffee. I shouted and turned to look at the rest of the group. Aloora's violet aura wasn't moving. Gunther was moving slowly, either dwarves weren't affected as much or perhaps he had some sort of charm that counteracted elvish spells. I could hear coughing and my chest felt tight, the smoke was clogging up my airways. I held my breath and focused on willing myself to move against the spell that was holding me.

The security guards were shouting in confusion, it sounded like they couldn't move at all. I heard Lorandir shout "Sheld!" and his forest green aura started to move towards the others. I shouted the same and felt the buzz of my magic surround me as my own protection charm activated. I could move, slower than I'd like, but at least I was moving. The others caught on and activated their own protection charms, but it looked like they were moving slowly too.

One of the elves had picked up the dagger and put it into a bag. The golden glow of the Dagger's aura was muted and had a greenish haze over it. I guessed the bag had been spelled to conceal items, but the Dagger's aura was too strong to be completely hidden.

There was more shouting. It sounded like museum security had arrived but couldn't enter either because of the smoke, which seemed to be getting thicker, or the spell that had held us.

The elves were on the move now. The one with the Dagger ran and somehow managed to evade all the people outside the room and slipped away. I tried to yell, but the smoke made my voice hoarse and croaky. It was getting harder to breathe too and my voice cracked as I forced out the shout. I willed myself to be heard above the two alarms and the water that was still raining down from the sprinklers. It seemed as if Lorandir heard because I saw his green aura move towards the entrance.

I was moving too slowly to catch the elf who had run, but the other one was moving more cautiously. I approached from behind and raised Bane to swing at its leg. I wanted to stop him or her from escaping. I wasn't an expert markswoman and I could only see the swirling aura of the elf rather than the precise shape of its body. I was rewarded with a cry of pain before the elf turned and blasted me with an electric blue bolt of lightning that lit up the purple smoke.

I was thrown backwards and hit the podium which had held the Dagger hard. Pain shot through my back and I fell forward onto the ground clumsily. I lost my grip on Bane and heard it skid across the floor. The fall had winded me and I gasped for air as the elf limped towards me. My hands scrabbled on the wet tiles, trying to find my axe. Instead my fist closed on the strange ball that was emanating smoke. It felt metal to my hands and had an aura of trollish magic surrounding it. I whispered the Dwarfish word for stop, tracing the rune weakly with my finger onto the metal and willing my magic to override the trollish sorcery.

If it was made of anything other than metal, I don't think it would have worked but the ball seemed to sputter and then the smoke stopped. It was still hanging thick in the room, but it did seem to be getting thinner as it crept out of the doorway and wasn't replaced.

The elf seemed to realise something was wrong as it stared at me. As the smoke cleared slightly, I saw a strange metallic tube and glinting glass eyes under the hood. It reminded me of a large insect. That made no sense, maybe I had hit my head in the fall.

The elf hissed a word, and more blue lightning arced around it. I heard Gunther cry out somewhere to my right and felt pain as the electricity coursed through me. The last thing I saw was the room glowing blueish purple and the floor sparking as the electricity fizzed across the water. Then I passed out.

When I came to, there was still a hint of purple haze in the room. An unfamiliar face was hovering over mine and I tried to scream but my throat was still hoarse from the smoke. I blinked and registered the green paramedic uniform.

I sat up too quickly, and sparks formed in front of my eyes.

"Take it easy," the paramedic smiled, "you've had a bump to the head. You seem OK, but we should get you to the hospital to be sure." She helped me up and I held onto the empty podium next to me for balance. I was impressed the podium had stayed upright after I had been flung against it.

"No hospitals. I'm fine," I coughed, "don't even worry about it." I wasn't convincing anyone. I looked around the room. Gunther and Aloora had cups of hot drinks and were talking in hushed tones.

Marco was coughing up purple phlegm and looked pale. The two tourists and the museum worker who had been trapped in the room with us were in similar conditions. The Professor was talking urgently with two police officers. Lorandir was nowhere to be seen.

Aloora rushed over once she saw I was awake and hugged me. "That was awful. That smoke, I could hardly breathe and I couldn't see. It's gone, Ame. They have it." She was distraught. Gunther was right behind her and rubbed her on the back tenderly.

I blinked again. This was too much. Dzraking elves and dzraking dragons. Dzrak to everything! Dwarfish was definitely the best language for cursing and I felt slightly better after swearing in my head. My head was throbbing, there was a dull ache along my back where I had hit the podium and my leg was jerking uncontrollably, a reaction to the electrical magic bolt that I'd been blasted with.

A policewoman entered carrying a black mask with large glass eyepieces and a metallic tube attached to the front like a strange elephant. Gas masks. That made sense, the elves had planned to release the smoke. She placed it into a see-through evidence bag and placed it next to another one containing a crowbar. I was surprised that had been able to break bullet proof glass and guessed it had been enchanted.

The paramedic's interest in me was fading as she looked around the room. Thank you Lorandir. Aloora and Gunther took the opportunity to usher me past the officials in the room and into the lobby. I tried to hold my breath as a coughing fit threatened to take hold and I wasn't sure the spell could hide that. Tears leaked from my eyes, but we made it to the gift shop before I leaned against a wall and coughed, trying to catch the purple spit in my coat sleeve. I swore as whatever was in the smoke stained my pale sheepskin coat. I hoped it would come out in dry cleaning.

Lorandir spotted us and sauntered over gracefully. "They got away." His voice was dispassionate but a muscle in his cheek twitched.

"Espretha..." I muttered between coughs. Everyone looked at me. "I think it was the same elves that took Aloora…wanted to…redeem selves," I managed to sputter.

Gunther let out a low whistle. Aloora narrowed her eyes. Both of them seemed less affected than me and I wondered if full-blooded magical beings were better able to recover from the smoke.

"Marco…" My voice was croaky.

An expression of concern passed over Aloora's face. "He was passed out and frothing at the mouth when the smoke cleared. So were the tourists. I think it's best he goes with the paramedics."

I nodded and forced myself to stand up straighter. Gunther disappeared into the shop and reappeared moments later with a bottle of water. I swilled some around my mouth before I swallowed, the cool clear liquid soothing my throat.

"What now?" he asked. We all looked at each other. The elves had the Fang Dagger, and they clearly knew the location they were going after. There was only the ritual left to decipher and they would have what they wanted – a dragon.

The Professor approached, twirling his long moustache between a finger and thumb. He was accompanied by a very annoyed looking Mei.

"How did you know about this?" she hissed, "I've had to explain to a *very* important collector that his prized possession has been stolen despite all the extra security…and the police have no leads. So tell me how it is that you lot were here before I insist that you are arrested."

"I told you already, my dear…" The Professor began.

"Don't you dare "my dear" me Elrond. Start making sense," Mei used her fingers to emphasise her air quotes.

The Professor gave a small half bow and continued, “It is as we said yesterday, m...Mei. We think that a group of people are trying to awaken a dragon. They have a ritual. They kidnapped this young gnome here to help them translate it and they needed an artefact. Your display gave them an opportunity and now they are closer than before to being able to complete the ritual,” he paused. “Perhaps I should speak to your benefactor…”

Mei wagged a finger at him, “Oh no you don’t. What else do you know? How can we get it back?”

“Blood,” I croaked. Mei looked at me with wide brown eyes. I took another swig of water, “I mean, I cut one of the elves. He… She…it was bleeding.”

Mei nodded, “Yes, the police saw the blood trail and the bloody axe in the room. They didn’t know the weapon was yours though. They followed the trail and the dogs have been sniffing round, but it disappears just across the road. The working theory is they got into a car, they’re looking at CCTV and traffic cameras but nothing yet.”

My chest felt tight. The police had my axe. There was no way they’d release it while an active investigation was going on. Schiztz.

“So they’re keeping you informed?”

Mei rolled her eyes, “Obviously.”

“Will you keep us informed? We’re trying to stop them after all. Now that they have the dragon artefact, that is, the Fang Dagger, we should focus on the translation of the ritual. It will tell us more about what they plan to do and how they will do it. There might be a clue we can use to stop them.”

Mei sighed angrily, “Alright. But you promise to tell me what you translate in this damned ritual.” She wagged her finger at the Professor again then whirled off as he executed another half bow.

“Food I think!” he exclaimed and then called a taxi.

I stumbled back towards the exhibition room and Gunther put a hand on my shoulder. I turned to look at his questioning face.

"My axe…" I didn't need to say anymore. He knew the importance of dwarfish weapons and he also knew my father had gifted me our ancestral axe only a few short years ago. He shook his head sadly.

"I have to try," I replied and brushed him off. I made it back to the room. Marco and the other humans were already gone, presumably to the hospital. I scanned the room and saw my axe in a large evidence bag. I could try to grab it and run off, risking arrest and injury as everyone was tense after the robbery and more likely to be trigger happy…or I could do the mature thing and speak to the policewoman standing next to the table with the evidence on it. It was tempting, but I decided to be mature.

I explained that I owned the axe and yes I might have hit one of the culprits but I changed my story slightly, making out that I slipped on the water and I couldn't see anything. The policewoman noted down my story and frowned at the goggles hanging round my neck but didn't say anything about them.

"You'll have to file a statement. And we need to run some tests. That's evidence."

"Please," I squeaked.

Her face softened, "Give me your number and we'll be in touch when your axe can be released. I've got your statement, we'll let you know if we need anything else."

There was nothing more I could do and I walked dejectedly back to join the others. I wanted to be alone to wallow in self-pity but I had an overwhelming sense of duty to our group, committed to stopping a dragon from being woken up.

I didn't say anything as we climbed into the taxi and the Professor gave directions to a restaurant. I didn't really register Gunther taking my hand or rubbing my shoulder as we sat in the grey interior of the car. He might have been the only one who understood what having a weapon, an ancestral weapon, taken from a dwarf meant but I was too wrapped up in myself to even acknowledge him.

Chapter 12

The Professor took us to a restaurant on Albany Road that specialised in elvish food. It was filled with elves and a couple of humans who were living on the wild side and experiencing a different culture for the evening.

I hadn't been there before and, as I stared at the menu, I could barely keep the look of disgust off my face when I discovered it was mostly vegetarian or vegan. What a schiztz way to end a schiztz day.

A tall blonde elf arrived quickly to take our drinks orders and was delighted to see the Professor again so I guessed he was a regular. Professor Maron ordered for us from the limited drinks selection and soon a jug of fizzy spring water from the elvish city of Breconia and glasses of light honey wine were on the table.

I downed half of my wine in one go, I was depressed and wanted alcohol to salve my wounds. I ordered one of the speciality platters but was not expecting anything much. The Professor kept up an air of joviality with trivial small talk but the rest of us were downcast as we sipped our fizzy water in silence.

Aloora was texting Marco to make sure he was OK. Lorandir was brooding. Gunther looked angry and I was glum.

The smiling waitress brought our food orders quickly and I stared at my plate filled with greenish parcels. The speciality platter was looking like a big mistake. I shoved one of the dark green leaves into my mouth and immediately changed my mind. The leaf disintegrated and a rich creamy sauce filled my mouth; it was a pleasant combination of earthy and slightly sweet. Then I tasted the gamey flavour of deer stewed in spices. It was a perfect balance of flavours. I had seriously misjudged elvish cooking and began eating with a lot more relish. It was probably having something filling and savoury to eat rather than café cakes and sugary sweets, but I felt a little better as I ate.

The Professor finally registered the depressed silence at our table. "Now, now, young adventurers. We cannot give up. We still have the ritual to translate and with both Aloora and I working on it, we can get it done in half the time."

"But…" Gunther started.

"We must control what we can now. These dragon awakeners have a plan. We must try to stop them. The ritual is our only clue for now. We have already made good progress on the translation. Aloora, my dear, join me in my office tomorrow after a good night's sleep and we shall swiftly decipher the rest."

I tried to share the Professor's optimism but I was never really given to flights of fancy, despite my love of fantasy literature. The reality was that the elves had everything in their favour and we were relying on translating a print out of a ritual and a lot of guesswork around locations.

I kept that to myself and instead commented. "We need a better name for them than 'dragon awakeners'. That sounds like a weird yoga group or some sort of chat line."

Gunther snorted and sprayed his dish with the mouthful of fizzy water he had just gulped. The atmosphere lightened considerably after that. I forced myself to stay engaged as we each came up with more outrageous suggestions for what to call this group of idiots intent on raising monsters.

"The Dragonettes!"

"Dragonateers! All for one and one for all!"

"Dragonistas!"

"Draconic raisers!" We all stared at the Professor after he made that suggestion then burst into laughter.

I wheezed, "That sounds like a metal band." Images of head banging elves appeared in my mind and it was so incongruous with the usual image of a graceful elf, I laughed even more.

We passed through more abstract suggestions - Woke being among them - before eventually we settled on *The Awakeners.* I still thought it sounded a bit like a student band but I couldn't come up with anything better. We finished the meal in a lot better mood than we started and I was grateful the Professor had dragged us out.

He paid the bill with a flourish, batting aside all offers of contributions from the rest of us. As we prepared to leave, he pulled me to one side.

"I know what your axe means to you, adventurer, but trust to the universe and you will have it when you need it," he gave me a theatrical wink at the end before turning to say goodbye to the others. I had no idea how to respond to that. I'm not into trusting the universe and the Professor's platitudes grated on me. I felt uncomfortable for the duration of the taxi ride home, the unease at losing my axe settling on me again after the fun at the meal.

Weapons are important to dwarves, treated with respect and reverence. My axe had been passed down from generation to generation, an unbroken tradition from all those ancestors who had wielded it or displayed it on their walls. I had let them all down, I had let my dad down. I couldn't even imagine how I could break the news to him. Er Dad, well you know that super important axe you handed me for safekeeping, passing on the traditions of my dwarven heritage, yeah well I was stupid enough to have it confiscated by the police and I might never get it back.

I shouted and screamed into my pillow until I was exhausted, then fell asleep.

Chapter 13

I awoke early the next day and took a disgruntled Errol for a walk. He snapped as we stepped out into the cool morning but I needed to burn off some energy. I quickened my pace as I passed the stone animals leering over the wall that marked the boundary of Bute Park, probably some fancy of the former owner of Cardiff Castle. The animals looked ready to pounce as they peered down from the wall and the glass eyes gave them a sinister realism that always made me uneasy. The baboon in particular made me shudder as I passed it. I relaxed a little once I was inside the park, moving at a relaxed pace as I coaxed Errol along the path.

As I was trying to distract myself by paying attention to the trees budding into bloom and the soothing sound of the river Taff in the background, flowing fast after the recent rain. Aloora texted me uncharacteristically early. She was heading to the Professor's office and Marco had been discharged from hospital already. He was sleeping but might like a call later.

I was about to make a mental note but decided instead to set a reminder on my phone. The more grating sounds of the city waking up and traffic on the road started to get louder and I headed for home, stopping at the Dragon's Head coffee shop on the way for a filling bacon sandwich. Errol started pulling me along as soon as we left the shop as he hurried to get back into the warmth of the forge.

There was nothing to do but wait for news of the translation. I killed time between customers by searching for news of dragons on my phone but didn't come up with anything useful. Searching for dragons and castles pulled up images of dragon motifs and an interesting legend that there was a dragon sleeping under Castell Coch. I saved it for later and sent the link to the rest of our group. I got a strange eye roll emoji back from Gunther I wasn't sure he had meant to send and radio silence from everyone else.

My reminder to call Marco beeped just as I was closing the shop. I jumped as the alarm broke the silence of the Arcade before realising what it was. It took me several moments to turn it off and I apologised to Errol who was peering blearily into the room, his sleep disturbed by the noise. Eventually, I managed to turn off the alarm, cursing definitely helped, and call Marco. He sounded very happy when he answered, although a bit hoarse, and I asked how he was.

"Yes I am doing very well. Aloora has gone to see the Professor of course but she left me some chocolates and the lovely Lorandir has been caring for me. He is very attentive you know and he has found this divine elvish tea, I feel so much better," I smirked at the idea of the elf being a house maid.

"Do you want me to come over?"

"No, no. Don't you dare! It's just me and Lorandir tonight, he has promised to cook me some soup for my throat and I have promised to show him *Lord of the Rings*, can you believe he hasn't seen it?!"

I frowned. I couldn't believe anyone hadn't seen it. "OK, well I'll leave you two to it then. I'll come over later in the week."

"Yes, yes. Now I say goodbye," As he hung up, I thought I could hear him greeting Lorandir. It sounded like they were going to have a cosy evening.

I decided to make some noodles and do some work in the forge. I needed to replenish my stock of protection charms and I wanted to keep busy. Even though I didn't usually have Bane on my person, the empty shelf under my distressed counter had weighed on me all day.

My phone buzzed while I was eating. Mum and Dad. Schiztz. I ignored them and scoffed the rest of my noodles before heading downstairs. Errol had perked up a bit after sulking from his enforced early morning walk and sat in my lap as I worked, lending his heat to help when I needed it and being a comforting warming presence.

I went to bed late but still couldn't sleep. I guiltily texted my Dad to tell him I hadn't heard the phone ring as I was busy making jewellery and was going to bed now. I promised to call them later in the week. Well I'd call them if I wasn't killed when a cult raised a dragon. I stared at the ceiling for a long time, studying a strange grey stain in the shape of a leaf, or a heart I supposed if I was more romantic. I decided to watch something and set up my laptop to play a Marvel movie marathon while I raided my emergency chocolate stash and idly managed to get through a family sized bar of Cadbury's Dairy Milk Caramel. I woke up the next day with the laptop still playing and when I went to the bathroom, I found the chocolate wrapper was stuck to my cheek. Classy!

I spent most of the next two days going for long walks with Errol, who was looking leaner at the enforced exercise despite regular stops at the Dragon's Head for bacon sandwiches, hot chocolates and cakes. I also worked on my jewellery, building up my stock. Customers seemed to be few and far between and I rushed through my store of metals and gems in a bid to distract myself. I'd just called Gunther to order more precious metal, when the tell-tale beep of a text message came through. Almost in unison we said "Aloora," Gunther summarised for me as I fumbled with my phone's buttons.

"She and the Professor have finished the translation. They're at the Professor's office. Come at once!"

"That's great news!" I glanced at the clock behind my counter. "I'll close up early and be there soon."

"Meet you there…bring your order if you like, business continues after all!" Gunther hung up.

I took a few minutes to get ready. I decided not to bring Errol, he was a bit grumpy if he was woken up after a long walk, and this morning we'd romped around Bute Park for over an hour, I'd enjoyed the crisp morning air and Errol had chased some pigeons. I left my goggles on my head by accident and didn't notice until I was halfway to the University. I took them off to shove in my pocket, got annoyed with the strap dangling out and worried I would lose them so ended up putting them back on my head. I was really decisive sometimes.

I steeled myself as I passed through the University gates, speeding up and glancing from side to side as I crossed the car park. No wyrms appeared and I rushed into the main building. Maybe the pack of wyrms had moved on but I couldn't help feeling nervous every time I was in that car park. The same security guard was on the front desk as I entered the University building.

"Don't you ever go home?" I asked with a smile as I signed in.

"I could say the same to you lovely. What are you doing back here again?"

"Meeting Professor Maron."

"You and half the world it seems," he grinned with a shake of his head at the Professor's visitor schedule.

My phone beeped and I saw an impatient text from Aloora asking where I was. “Got to go,” I gave a wave and headed up the stairs.

There was an empty chair for me as I arrived. Everyone else had managed to get to the Professor’s office before me which made me wonder exactly where Gunther had been. His office was by the railway station so he should have been further away than me.

I waved stupidly as I entered. Marco was the only one who waved back. He had a pastel blue scarf wound round his throat, complimenting his dark blue jumper. His chair was pushed close to Lorandir’s, who looked a little worn out. Marco was a demanding patient I guessed.

The Professor clapped his hands together as I sat down. “Excellent! Now our intrepid group is back together, young Aloora and I have a translation to share. Shall you do the honour or shall I?”

Aloora graciously gestured towards the Professor and he held up a notebook with a flourish. It felt a bit wrong that he was about to read an ancient ritual and it was inscribed in a plain white spiral bound notebook, especially as we were surrounded by books and parchments that were probably older than he was.

He spoke in an ancient language that sounded dark and mysterious. I thought I felt magic as he read and pulled my goggles over my eyes in time to see a strange golden red power. It was faint, but it still made the hairs on my neck prickle. The reading was finished surprisingly quickly and the Professor beamed round at us. Marco shuddered. I wasn’t the only one who felt power in the room, even if he couldn’t see it.

“What does it mean?” Gunther was frowning, he was more sensitive to magic than I was.

“Arise, slumbering one” The Professor began dramatically. “Arise o slumbering serpent. Return your power to this world. We channel the power of this dragon and offer the gift of fresh blood. We ask for your protection. We offer you our flesh. Return to this world. Arise slumbering one."

It sounded like exactly the sort of bloody ritual that a cult would use, although it lost some of its menace in English.

"That's it?" I asked with some disbelief, it was short for something that had the potential to be so devastating.

Aloora nodded. "It's short but it could work. Did you feel the power when it was read in Draconic? Even without intent it's powerful, which means we got the translation right. We were a bit confused by "this dragon", it could mean the dragon that is sleeping but more likely it's a reference to the artefact they're planning on using. The Fang Dagger."

"And "flesh" is used here in the context of offering servitude rather than literally. It sounds like they want to worship the dragon, which means it's likely from the ancient dragon cult of Mulath-ta. I thought all of their rituals had been destroyed but somehow this one has survived," the Professor finished. They both looked proud of themselves, it had clearly taken a lot of work to get this done.

"Well done!" I said. It came out more sarcastic than I meant so I hurried on as Aloora narrowed her eyes at me and the Professor looked amused. "So what now?"

"Excellent question," the Professor beamed at me, a little condescendingly, I thought. "Now we have to make sure they cannot use it. Without the translation, they won't know exactly what intent to put into the ritual so we are one step ahead of them. Of course, if we could find their location and put a stop to this whole thing, that would be better."

Knowing what the ritual meant was a big step forward and Aloora and the Professor were excited at the discovery of a lost Mulath-ta ritual, but it didn't feel like we were ahead to me. I clamped my mouth shut. For the first time in days, a mood of optimism gripped the group and I wasn't going to let my cynicism ruin it.

While Marco and Lorandir congratulated the translators, I motioned to Gunther then stood by the door. I handed him my order list. He squinted.

"You need to improve your handwriting," he remarked bluntly. It wasn't like him so I guessed he was as cynical as I was about how far this translation put us ahead.

I shrugged, "I can email it." Gunther nodded.

A thought struck me, "Is there a way I can enchant metal or gems so they can be found by someone?"

He tilted his head, considering. I decided to be honest. "It's an idea I've been having, ever since I saw Espretha's charm….Lorandir!" I shouted. Everyone turned to look at me then. I felt my face heating so ploughed on.

"Er, the charm you used to find Espretha, can you use it again?"

They all turned to look expectantly at him now. He shook his head and replied somewhat defensively. "I have been trying. She's shielding her location from me, I think she wants to sever her connection with me, but unless both charms are destroyed, she can't entirely."

He sounded so miserable that I was sorry I'd brought it up. "Sorry," I apologised. He shrugged and turned back to the Professor to discuss the translation again.

"Nice try love," Gunther patted my shoulder, "I'll have a think about how you could enchant the metal. It might be able to be done…" He got a thoughtful look on his face and he stroked his well-kept beard. I needed to speak to a master craftsdwarf really, my Dad might know, but I was still avoiding his calls in case he asked about my axe.

I wandered home slowly, still underwhelmed with the translation and depressed from losing my axe. I was re-reading a fantasy novel in my shop, when my phone rang. I didn't recognise the number and answered warily.

"Hello?"

"Good Morning. Is that Ms Haernson?" The voice sounded clinical and put me on my guard. No one called me Ms Haernson.

"Speaking."

"It's Sergeant Davies. I believe we have something of yours. An… axe?" The professional lady on the other end of the phone sounded a bit surprised. "Yes, an axe. Well we're ready to release it if you'd like to come and pick it up."

Shock made me less eloquent than usual. "Er…yes…er…right away…please."

I took down the address and practically raced out of the door. As I did so, I got a call from Aloora. That was unusual, she normally messaged me on one of her many social media apps.

"We've got a lead!" She practically screamed down the phone. "Meet at the Professor's office."

"I'll be there soon," my voice choked, "I'm picking up my axe."

I imagined Aloora looking at the phone with a bemused expression before she hung up. I practically ran to the police station. I arrived out of breath with frizzy hair puffing up. I tried to slow my breathing and sauntered up to the police desk.

The officer on duty gave me a look that said he knew I was guilty of something, but couldn't be bothered to write it up…unless I made his life difficult.

"I'm here to collect an axe," I didn't know how to make that sound better so tried my best to look as dwarfish as possible. The officer raised an eyebrow and sighed before pointedly checking his computer. I'd just made his morning difficult. He blinked and read the screen twice. I imagined the report didn't look good so kept quiet with what I hoped was a bright friendly smile on my face.

"Name?" I gave it to him and without being prompted, held up my driver's licence. I didn't own a car but at times like this I was very glad my parents had insisted on me learning and getting the proper paperwork. Dwarves and humans alike respected paperwork, well, most of the time.

The officer studied it, checking the flat-haired young woman in the picture against the fluffy-haired red-faced one who was at his desk. I gave him a smile and he decided it matched.

He called another officer over to watch the desk then walked to get my axe. It was in an evidence bag and still had dried blood on it when he brought it back. He placed it carefully on the desk and gave me a form to sign. I read it through carefully then signed with a flourish. I reached up to take the bag tentatively, watching the officer's face for any sign he might change his mind. He just nodded then went back to the computer. I grabbed it, ripped the bag open and only just stopped myself from hugging the axe, which given it was large, double-headed and razor sharp would just have looked odd. I walked out of that station a lot happier than I had gone in.

I practically skipped on the way to Professor Maron's office, I even stopped for a doughnut from one of the many Gregg's shops in the city. I got excellent if somewhat nervous service, possibly due to my wide grin or the axe I'd shoved into my jeans, or both.

I arrived in time to see Marco and Lorandir walking up the university steps, arms linked. I shouted and ran over and gave Marco a hug. Seeing the shock on his face, I laughed and spun him round. Then I hugged Lorandir for the joy of having my ancestral axe back, I didn't try to spin him round though and he hugged me awkwardly in return. I caught them exchanging looks as if I'd gone mad but I didn't care. I was ecstatic and couldn't hide the bounce in my step or my massive smile as I signed in and rushed up the stairs.

I saw Gunther and pulled the axe from my trousers. "I got it back!" I exclaimed, waving it a little too enthusiastically. He grinned back at me, nodding, he truly understood the importance of the weapon.

"I am glad to see you have your axe back young half-dwarf, I knew Chief Inspector Marbles would come through. Perhaps we could put it away now? I just got a concerned call from the security office."

I turned to look at the Professor, "You? You got my axe back?"

He shrugged elegantly, "I merely spoke to the Chief Inspector. He's very interested in dragons you know, I met him at some university event. I told him our suspicions too of course but really his hands are tied without more evidence. Your axe on the other hand…"

"Thank you. I can never repay you enough," I crossed the room, stepping over piles of books and papers to reach him. I offered him my hand, then grasped his wrist in a traditional dwarfish greeting of comrades when he reached out to shake hands. I hugged him for good measure. He seemed very pleased with that and twirled his moustache delightedly after I released him.

"It seems we have two reasons to celebrate. The return of your weapon, and…a lead!"

I had practically forgotten the lead Aloora had mentioned.

The Professor's optimism and my buoyant mood seemed to lift everyone and I beamed as the Professor filled us in. He had been contacted by one of his PhD students about a tricky translation in Draconic. When pressed, he had disclosed that he had been offered money for translating it quickly and had the impression it was important so wanted to check his reading of it with the Professor before going back to his clients. Professor Maron was wily, he'd managed to get the time and location of their meeting point to exchange the translation. I didn't fully understand why they weren't emailing the translation, but maybe cults were paranoid about the internet.

The Professor had also put some doubts in the student's mind about the meaning of the runes so the intent wouldn't be as clear as if the cult had a direct translation. It sounded strangely nuanced to me, but Aloora was nodding along. So all we had to do was be at the appointed meeting place – The Goat – early and try to stop whoever met them.

Chapter 14

The meeting time was one p.m., and I was nervous. I was waiting in Marco's small car with Lorandir in case the student was meeting Espretha and her magic-wielding companion. The others were already in The Goat, I hoped acting normally, but Marco had seemed very excitable this morning. I was a bit leery of how he'd manage to fit in amongst the supernatural patrons, but he'd insisted on going saying he wanted to see the décor of the magical pub in person.

I had moved the pine air freshener out of the way and had used my goggles to try to see who might be in the pub but it was tricky as we couldn't park directly outside and instead were on double yellow lines on the main road, Castle Street. I couldn't see any elvish auras but had spotted a group of goblins going in and a pixie, who looked shiftily from side to side before heading down the side street that led to The Goat. Lorandir's forest green aura was glowing brightly in the passenger seat next to me and, combined with the pungent pine scent, was giving me a headache so I quickly gave up on the goggles.

He was looking moodily out of the window and kept flexing his legs, his tall frame fitting uncomfortably into the tiny Volkswagen. Car horns kept blaring as they passed us on the road, we were halfway on the pavement with the hazards on and the warning triangle set up behind us to give the illusion that we had broken down, but we were still blocking the Saturday afternoon traffic. One van driver rolled down his window to yell. "You can't park there love!"

I shrugged and gave him a winning smile. "Just waiting for recovery," I mouthed. Then I made a rude gesture, careful to keep my hand below the window in case he saw and came back. Mature, I know. Lorandir snorted at my childish behaviour and I responded by cranking the volume up on the radio. Unfortunately it was stuck on BBC Radio 4 because Marco believed it helped him learn English and the radio had broken after he had tuned it in. I quickly turned it back down as the presenter began a detailed discussion about the best way to dress a chicken for the oven on The Food Programme.

A blue Ford pulled up behind us, put on its hazard lights and the driver got out, to more beeps from the traffic. I held my breath, but it didn't seem like they were coming over to offer to help.

"You should get out and pretend to look at the engine," I told Lorandir. He gave me a look.

"You're the dwarf, you look at the engine," typical elvish stereotyping. I rolled my eyes.

"It's raining. I'm not getting out!" We left it at that.

I texted Aloora for news. She sent back a bored emoji. For something to do, I looked up the sunset times in Cardiff on my smartphone's browser, then set my phone alarm for 18:21. I was scrolling through alarm sound choices, annoying Lorandir who glanced my way irritably, before settling on the standard setting.

A few minutes later Aloora called. I muted the radio, now talking about how to get the perfect roast potatoes. It seemed like a complex series of steps involving fluffing potatoes, allowing them to cool and then roasting in goose fat. There was another chef on the line who was arguing with the method and claiming that dripping was in fact the best roasting fat to use. They had just started a debate about cooking times when I put her on speaker.

“He got away, running out now! Hoody! Follow him!”

“There!” Lorandir pointed out of the window at a tall figure in a black hoodie running to the car that had parked behind us.

Schiztz. The Ford tried to pull out into the traffic without indicating and I pulled out too. I thought I’d managed to block the car but it pulled out further and got round us, to the sound of many angry horns sounding. The driver tried to pull off but was stuck in Cardiff traffic. It was the slowest car chase in history as we moved along Castle Street. Lorandir’s hand twitched and I knew he was thinking about jumping out of the car. A gap opened up and I zoomed into it, waving a hasty thank you to the driver who had unwillingly let me out. At least we were moving.

I focused on following the car. I’d seen in films that you had to let other cars get between you if you were following another vehicle so it wasn’t too suspicious so I let a red sports car out.

“What are you doing?” Lorandir exclaimed, exasperated.

“That’s how you tail someone in the films,” I replied, squinting through the windscreen, “Just keep an eye on the blue Ford and tell me if it turns.”

He muttered something under his breath but watched the car intently, while I concentrated on staying behind the sports car and not letting anyone else in between us. I got the finger from a van driver for my trouble and resisted the urge to swear at him under the dashboard as I blinked out through the windscreen, the rain getting heavier. Marco’s windscreen wipers staggered back and forth across the glass as I struggled to see in the downpour. He really needed to get his car serviced.

At that point he rang. I shoved my phone at Lorandir. Next, I heard Marco's voice shouting about his car and where were we. I called out that we were crossing the river and I'd bring it back as soon as we found anything. I heard a string of Italian. I grabbed the phone, held it up to my mouth and made crackling sounds.

"Sorry…breaking….up..." then I hung up on him. Lorandir stared at me.

"What? You've never pretended you didn't have signal? Look at the road!"

He returned to staring out of the window, then pointed. The blue car had turned right and was motoring along the edge of Bute Park. The traffic lights were already on amber. I accelerated through. We narrowly avoided the oncoming traffic which had just started to roll forwards as their lights changed. We were now directly behind the car. Schiztz. This wasn't covered by any of the police shows I had watched with Mum.

Traffic was steady and although the driver of the blue car tried to overtake several times, it was too busy to get a clear gap and instead they tailgated the silver estate car in front of them. I hung back cautiously in case there was an accident, and trying not to look as if I was following it.

Suddenly, the blue car swerved out onto the other side of the road. An oncoming Ford Focus crashed up onto the pavement to avoid it, hitting a bollard for their trouble. The silver estate braked hard. I followed suit. Marco's brakes squealed loudly in protest. We stopped a centimetre away from the bumper. Lorandir started unbuckling his seatbelt.

Pedestrians were already crowding around the damaged Ford and the driver was on the pavement. Others had their phones out, calling the emergency services.

"What are you doing?" I practically screamed at the poor elf. The silver car started tentatively moving forward. I followed. I didn't dare to try to overtake as a fluorescent police car drove past in the opposite direction, lights flashing.

We caught up to the blue car at the next set of traffic lights. The driver had decided not to risk a collision or arrest by running the lights. The silver car turned slowly and we were once again behind the blue car.

The car continued following the road, crossing the river Taff again as we headed into some of the more residential areas. I ran a red light to keep behind it, frantically apologising as I sped past other drivers.

At the Coryton roundabout, the blue car dived into a small gap. Several other cars pulled out and I was forced to brake hard to avoid crashing. Lorandir grabbed the 'oh schiztz' handle on his side of the car tightly but kept quiet as I swore. I thought we'd lost the car but then they went past us again, going round the roundabout another time. We were in luck. I saw it take an exit. I followed with two cars between us. Lorandir pointed at the exit sign. We were going to Castell Coch. The name didn't seem quite so funny this time.

Chapter 15

Unsurprisingly given the weather, the car park was pretty empty with only a few family estates parked up, forcing fun on their children even in the rain.

As we pulled up, the dull red of the castle walls rising out from the green forest surrounding it made me pause. It looked like a fairy tale castle, with its round turrets and pointed roofs, it looked like it belonged in a romance novel or a kit book of how to build a medieval castle. It was hard to believe we were so close to the city.

I saw an indistinct tall figure in a hoody striding towards the castle entrance. I guessed it was the same figure we had followed here but couldn't be sure with the rain now pelting down and making everything blurry. Marco's windscreen wipers seemed to have finally given up after being on the highest setting for all of forty minutes.

Lorandir was already out of the door heading towards the entrance while I was texting the others the news and reassuring Marco his car was alright, although it definitely needed a service. Who could own a car without working windscreen wipers in Wales of all places?

I cursed to myself before heading out into the rain and sprinting over the wooden drawbridge to the shelter of the entrance. Lorandir was waving two tickets at me and we walked in without any trouble. The rain and Lorandir's enchantments making it tricky to see our weapons. I tried to avoid fingering my axe nervously as we walked through the arched entrance into the castle courtyard.

I pretended to study the building as if deciding where to go first whilst staying dry under the arch. The bricks were a dusky red and accented the vibrant fire-engine red gothic style wooden walkways. I glanced at the map Lorandir had given me. Apparently the current picturesque exterior was created by the Marquess of Bute but underneath was a thirteenth century castle.

The hooded figure was nowhere to be seen, but it made sense to go down, after all the dragon was meant to be slumbering underneath the ground, otherwise it would have been disturbed when all of the Victorian building work had gone on to create the fairy tale confection we were standing in. I elbowed Lorandir, who was glaring at the castle as if it could tell us where the figure had gone, and pointed at the dungeon on the fold out map before heading off in that direction. He overtook me after a few steps and quickly covered the open courtyard to the passage that led to the dungeon.

We walked past the doorway to the dungeon slash cellar three times before noticing the glamour that had been placed over it to make it less interesting to visitors. We were in the right spot. I wondered why Gunther's anti-illusion charm hadn't allowed me to see through it straight away, then put the question out of my mind for another time.

I felt a tingle and a sense of strange elven magic washed over us as we passed through the doorway. It was a strange sensation, a bit like feeling long dry grass brushing against my body combined with fire and it passed quickly as we entered the room. It wasn't like any other elven magic I had experienced, but then it wasn't like I'd really had close contact with many elves before this week.

The space was surprisingly light for being underground with large yellow stones lending a sense of age to the room. In one corner, those stones had been moved away, revealing the entrance to a dark tunnel.

The entranceway was large enough for me to walk through standing up but not an elf. I crouched to one side, careful not to silhouette myself in the entrance. I studied the tunnel closely but couldn't tell if it was dwarven or manmade. The stones had been taken out methodically from this one spot and placed against the wall. They knew exactly where this passage was. A thought struck me. They hadn't bothered to cover it up again. Either they were coming back this way or they were confident they wouldn't be followed or…this was a trap.

Staying crouched to one side, I took out my phone, turned on the torch setting and shone it down the tunnel. I could just see the regular wooden supports and uneven stone floor. It smelled damp and there was green moss growing on the walls and underfoot. It didn't look like it was well used.

I shared my thoughts with Lorandir. He looked uncomfortable when I mentioned it could be a trap, but stoically replied "We don't have a choice do we? We've got to try to stop them."

He glanced uneasily at the tunnel before drawing his sword and stepping inside. He had to walk with his knees bent and shoulders hunched to avoid hitting the roof of the tunnel. It was an odd stance and he looked like a strange insect, all angles and joints.

I tried my phone. One bar. I sent a text to Aloora letting them know where we were.

Found tunnel in dungeon at castle cock. Following it. I sent it before I clocked the autocorrect changes. Oh well. I paused before I entered the tunnel and thought longingly of my quiet jewellery shop. I could turn back and ignore this. Then I thought of the culs who had kidnapped my friend and of the damage a rampaging dragon could cause. I knew I didn't really have a choice either.

We still had a couple of hours before sunset, but Lorandir was right. I sighed, gripped my axe tightly and followed him. The light disappeared quickly in the dank tunnel. My night vision was pretty good thanks to my Dad's dwarven genes but this was pitch black without the phone. I shone my torch down to avoid tripping on the uneven stone floor.

I caught up with Lorandir at the first roof strut. He was rubbing his head and swearing in Elvish. I was thankful for my short build in this tunnel. Jutting out from the ancient beam was a strange iron loop, I looked at it for a few seconds before realising it was to hold torches. This had once been in regular use then, although the Awakeners had not been considerate enough to light the way today.

I chivalrously offered to go first but he shook his head and crouched lower to avoid overhead beams.

The passage sloped gently downwards and looked like it was in good condition from what I observed of the wooden supports as we passed them. The air was warmer in the tunnel and it was clammy, undisturbed for goodness knows how long, it seemed oppressive somehow. I shuddered.

We were silent by unspoken mutual consent and on edge. I was focusing on avoiding a puddle that had formed on the floor of the tunnel when Lorandir stopped so quickly that I bumped into him. I was about to swear when he whispered urgently.

“I heard something ahead,” I nodded even though he couldn’t see me. I hesitated for a moment trying to work out if it was better to shine my phone in that direction or turn it off. I decided that whatever it was had probably already seen us so aimed the torchlight to the side of Lorandir’s slim frame. It didn’t do a lot to illuminate the passage. I got the vague sense of a more cavernous area ahead but that was it.

Lorandir edged forward and I kept my phone and my axe up.

Less than a hundred paces along the tunnel, an opening appeared on either side making an underground crossroads. We stopped and looked into the side tunnels cautiously. I shone my phone around the intersection.

The tunnel cutting across the one we were walking down didn’t look like it had been constructed in a structured way. There were no wooden struts holding up the frame of the tunnel, no stones or wooden boards on the floor, just dirt. I knelt down and picked some up. It looked like the dirt had been packed down by the weight of something heavy but somehow it still looked fresh.

I stood and shone my phone’s torch upwards at the roof. It was taller than the passage we were traversing and was curved. It had the same look of being packed in as the floor. I heard a slithering sound behind us. As it moved closer, the sound grew into some sort of chewing noise mixed with a rumbling movement. The ground shook slightly. Dirt trickled from the roof of the passage.

Both Lorandir and I whirled around to see a large white shape coming through the new tunnel towards us. He grabbed my arm and pulled me back into our original tunnel. We staggered back as the thing undulated past us. I shone my torch onto it, illuminating its moist greyish white skin. I couldn’t see anything more as it took up the entire passageway. The tunnel shook as it passed through, bunching its muscles to move itself forward.

"What is that?!"

"A goliath," I quietly named the large worm-like creatures that were the bane of dwarfish mines across Europe. I hadn't ever seen one as they didn't like too much noise or light so kept away from tunnelling close to the main dwarven underground centres. I had seen pictures in books though. I hoped it was just passing through.

Its body was at least the length of three buses and it took some time to go through the passage. After what seemed like an age, its stubby grey-blueish tail passed us and it disappeared from sight.

I sighed with relief, "Let's get out of here."

We had moved about twenty paces when I heard that slithering sound again. It was moving faster this time. With mouths open, we turned. This time the goliath didn't carry along its own tunnel but turned into the passage we were in. By the dim light of my phone, I saw rows of sharp teeth coming towards us, oozing with blue saliva.

We ran. It followed, moving quickly as it bunched and released its muscles. I stumbled on a loose cobblestone and fell, crying out automatically. The goliath heard me and slowed as if it was scenting the air. I tried to stand quietly. The noise of pushing myself up was enough. It lunged. I tried to move backwards but was too close to the tunnel wall. Backed against it, I flung my arms up in automatic defence and fell to the ground again.

It stopped and backed up a little.

"The light!" Lorandir shouted. My phone's torch was shining directly at the goliath, throwing the creature's long pointed teeth into sharp relief. Each one was as long as my forearm and the rows of teeth went back into its body as far as I could see. I angled the phone higher, aiming for where I thought the eyes were, four bulbous black globes sunk into its head above its maw.

It retreated further but wasn't going away. While it was focused on me, Lorandir had edged along the other side of the tunnel, his sword ready to strike. When he was close enough, he swung and his sword sunk easily into the goliath's grey skin. It roared in pain and turned to look at the elf.

I pushed myself up and ran towards it, heaving my axe upwards to strike at its exposed lower jaw. Now it was really pissed off. It roared again, the tunnel vibrated with its power and dirt sprinkled down onto my hair. I leapt backwards with agility I didn't know I possessed to avoid its massive head as it turned towards me.

Lorandir had a dagger in his left hand and threw it deftly. It struck one of the goliath's glittering eyes and sunk deep. The creature thrashed in pain, shrieking horribly as its head banged up and down against the tunnel's edges. It succeeded in driving the dagger in deeper and screamed again.

It began moving backwards in what I thought was a retreat. I staggered to Lorandir who had one hand against the wall supporting himself. A chunk of earth fell onto my face and I pushed the dirt out of my eyes, ready to make a snarky comment when the ground started shaking.

My head snapped round to look at the goliath…where the goliath had been. With a surprising turn of speed, it had burrowed down into the tunnel floor, chewing through the chunky cobblestones as if they were nothing. Schiztz. The ground was now seriously unstable and I backed up without thinking. Lorandir stepped in the opposite direction, waving me forward along the tunnel.

The floor of the passage shifted beneath my feet and the goliath roared as it entered the tunnel anew, pushing the earth up furiously.

It angled itself to lunge towards Lorandir, the direction it was expecting us to be. I heard a grunt and the sound of metal grinding. I hoped that meant he was alright and still fighting.

I felt the weight of Bane in my hand and leaped as high as I could. I managed to get about two foot off the ground before I swung the axe down and into the back of the goliath. Blue blood spurted from the fresh cut and the creature twisted in pain. I was flung against the tunnel wall and I heard my axe clatter on the stones. Purple stars sparked in front of my eyes but I blinked past them and pushed myself to my feet, fighting a wave of nausea at standing too fast.

The creature was trying to turn to face me but the tunnel was too small for it to manoeuvre well. I shone my phone, searching for Bane and stumbled towards it, only a couple of steps away. The goliath screamed again, hopefully Lorandir had got a hit in too.

It managed to retreat into its tunnel sufficiently to squash its head down and turn to face me. I held up my phone desperately aiming it at its eyes. Only two remained. It reared away from the light but was determined. It bunched its muscles and I gripped my axe ready to go down fighting. Before it had the chance to strike, Lorandir appeared on its head. I was so shocked by his sudden appearance, my phone shifted downwards and the creature roared in triumph.

Lorandir positioned his sword between its two remaining eyes and plunged it in at the same time that the goliath lunged forward. I ran backwards, trying to get the light back in its eyes. I tripped over the uneven floor and fell. The goliath spasmed and I saw it bearing down on me. I closed my eyes, screamed and lifted my arm before I felt it land on my legs hard.

I cried out in pain and felt my legs sink into the tunnel floor, the dirt compacting down under the massive creature's weight.

I smelt its dank breath – aromas of mildew and mould spewed from it. I opened my eyes. I saw rows and rows of jagged long teeth. I screamed. After a while, I stopped screaming. I was still alive.

Lorandir had managed to stay atop of the creature as it had collapsed. He yanked his sword out of the burst eye and wiped it on the goliath, leaving blue streaks on its pale grey hide. He leapt down effortlessly to my side. I tried to wriggle out from under the creature's maw.

"You couldn't have killed it before it reached me?" I couldn't help myself.

He snorted in what I thought was an un-elf like way. "Do you want some help?" He asked pointedly. I grunted. He went behind me and slipped his arms under mine before levering me out from under the creature. There was a small indent in the tunnel floor where my legs had been forced into the ground. Once upright, I tested my weight on my feet cautiously but other than being bruised, my legs felt alright. I was lucky, I didn't even want to speculate about how much that thing weighed.

I was covered with blueish slime. I looked ruefully at my pale sheepskin coat, now a disgusting blue colour and tried to brush off the goo. This only resulted in my hands getting sticky so I stopped.

"Are you OK?"

I had nearly been crushed by a goliath, was covered with gloopy saliva, and my coat was ruined. "Don't even worry about it," was my reply, "what are the chances the Awakeners still don't know we're here do you think?"

Lorandir looked up as if contemplating my question seriously. "I'd say slim to none," he snorted again then laughed, a genuine musical elvish laugh.

I gave him a smile, "Guess we'd better keep going then."

He offered me his hand to help me up the goliath with a mock bow, “M’lady.”

“M’gentleman,” I replied with another smile as I climbed up onto the corpse. It still took up most of the tunnel and I crouched as I tried to cross it without slipping on the blood. I slid down the other side and did a neat jump over the mound of earth it had pushed up when it burrowed through the floor. Lorandir leapt down gracefully.

We carried on more slowly as the passage continued to slope downwards. Every tiny noise made me look around skittishly. Lorandir grumbled about keeping the torch still and I bit back a sharp retort. Now we were moving again, we were both on edge, wondering if we were going to meet another monster. I jumped when I saw a skinny rat run past us, its feet splashing through the small puddles on the floor as it hurried out of our way. I grimaced and kept going, staying close to the elf.

The rat clambered up over a mound of dirt and through a narrow gap ahead. It looked like part of the tunnel had collapsed. A beam was angled diagonally across the passageway. Dirt had fallen either side of it and had completely blocked the tunnel on the right hand side. There was a small gap to the left, under the old beam. Lorandir pressed himself against the wall so I could get closer and shine the torch through. Avoiding some poisonous looking mushrooms that oozed from the wood, I held up the torch then poked my head into the small space. I saw a shape move and jumped back with a squeak. This tunnel was not helping the air of confidence and fearlessness I was trying to project.

I heard a chittering sound and something scampered away. I made a shuddering noise and looked again. Now the way was clear. I muscled my way into the space, crawling as quickly as I could using my elbows to pull me along so I could keep my phone up. I managed to dislodge some earth from the ceiling and held my breath as I expected to be crushed. Fortunately it wasn't too much and I continued wriggling through.

I gracelessly exited the tiny space when the mound of dirt gave way under my hand and I slipped onto my head in a puddle. For dzrak's sake. Coughing and spluttering out dirt, I pulled my way forward and fully out of the small space.

"Are you OK?" Lorandir's voice sounded muffled at the other end of the tunnel.

"Just dzraking great," I mumbled while attempting to shake mud off my face before I shouted. "Yeah, fine, just watch the end here. I'll hold the torch for you."

Lorandir's face was a mask of concentration as he crawled through the tunnel. He was slim and didn't hit the roof at all. At the end, the floor stayed intact for him and he executed a compact forward roll out of the tunnel. I don't think I've ever felt less graceful.

The rest of the passage's supports were solid and there were no more cave-ins as we continued along, alert for more monsters in the dark.

Eventually the floor levelled off and the passage became a little larger. Lorandir could stand upright and he looked a lot less like an awkward spider as he straightened and rolled his shoulders, enjoying the relative freedom of movement.

I glanced down at my phone, we had been walking for two hours and the constant use of the torch had taken its toll on my battery. I still had no signal, I had no idea if the others had tried to follow us into the passageway or not. I heard a skittering noise behind us and nudged the elf forward nervously, I hoped it was just rats scurrying in the darkness and not something else.

Chapter 16

As we moved along, the walls of the tunnel became sturdier, turning from dirt to large grey stones. I spotted an old iron brace on one of the support beams. This part of the tunnel had been maintained over the years.

The stones reminded me of a place I had been before, but I couldn't place it as I trailed my hand along the wall. The dwarves called it "speaking to the stones" but I had never really had a knack for it and preferred to focus on creating jewellery or forging weapons like my Dad. Still, I had a feeling they were trying to tell me something, if only I could understand them.

The tunnel had widened and we were walking side by side when we came to a split in the passage. Three tunnels branched out ahead of us. Each looked identical and equally unappealing. The middle one had a menacing feel to it. I walked to the left one, then the right and Lorandir did the same. I felt a faint movement of air on my face from the one on the right.

"I think this one leads outside," I whispered. Lorandir stood next to me. He almost looked like he was scenting the air.

"I think you're right," he pointed to the middle one, which we had both walked past. "I can smell smoke from this direction."

I stepped up to it. I had an urge to turn away and try another passage. I forced myself to stay close to it and sniffed. After a moment, I caught the whiff of smoke too. I rubbed my head, trying to think. Would the Awakeners want fire? Did dragons really breathe fire and if so, did that mean it was already awake?

I had already turned unthinkingly away from the tunnel when I caught a faint wisp of elvish magic. Another glamour spell? I experimented by moving Bane through the entrance to the middle passage. Nothing happened. I poked it further in and put my arm into the entrance. I felt a sensation as if long grass was brushing my body combined with fire. The same as the spell over the dungeon entrance at Castell Coch.

"Better go that way then," I replied with bravado, stepping all the way into the tunnel. Apart from the feeling of grass tickling me and intense heat, I didn't feel anything else. Lorandir followed. He didn't comment on the enchantment but frowned as if something was off and I wondered if he'd felt the same sensation as I did.

I experimented with turning my torch off, it was too dark to see much, even with my dwarfish night vision, but after a moment, I noticed a faint greenish glow. I looked around and saw the walls and ceiling were covered with something that was glowing. This was new. I reached out to touch it. It was some sort of slimy algae growing on the tunnel walls. It was almost beautiful, in a green kind of way. I rubbed my fingers together and saw the bioluminescent glow was on me too. I stared at my glowing hand in wonder.

Lorandir placed a hand on my elbow, breaking into my thoughts. I was proud of myself for not shrieking.

He whispered, "Can you see by the plant light? Best keep the torch off if we can," I nodded but didn't know if he saw me as he had already started moving forward. I trailed my hand along the wall, leaving a glowing trail across the stones. My hand was getting greener by the minute so I stopped, feeling both stupid and a little like a superheroine with radioactive powers.

We moved slowly and silently along the passage. The smoky smell intensified as we continued and then there was light. Old fashioned torches flared in the darkness, held in place by the iron loops I had seen earlier in the tunnel. Shadows flickered across the passageway. It looked ominous.

This was the right place then.

We stuck to the walls and edged cautiously towards the flames, trying to stay in the shadows. I was suddenly thankful that my pale coat was filthy, it blended more with the darkness and the dull stones. I peered into the room. It looked empty. I risked looking more closely. There were some boxes to one side of the entrance. Ordinary cardboard boxes. Electric security lights were dotted around the walls, but were switched off in favour of more torches lining the walls. Stone steps led up to a heavy door in one corner.

Apart from the flames spluttering around the room, it looked like a store room. I crept behind the boxes. I looked up at the vaulted ceiling and suddenly I remembered where I had seen this type of stone before. We were underneath Cardiff Castle. I pulled out my phone and willed it to have some signal. It didn't. I silently typed messages to Aloora on every messaging service I could think of and hoped they would get through.

As I typed, I heard the door swing open. I risked peeking round the boxes and saw several robed figures descending. Their faces were completely hidden by large hoods. I pulled my head back behind the boxes as one of them started to draw a complicated symbol on the ground. I noted that this figure was wearing combat boots. They got so close to the pile of boxes I was hiding behind that I could hear their laboured breathing as they crouched close to the ground with their chalk. I held my breath, biting my bottom lip as the figure passed and I heard it shuffle away.

I heard more footsteps and a sharp voice commanding everyone to hurry up. I noticed a gap between some boxes at the bottom of the stack and contorted myself into a ball to see through it. One of the figures held a wooden box, which they set in the centre of the drawing. The figure with the chalk was still walking around the room and irritably telling others to move as they worked to complete their markings. A tall figure stood in the very middle of the room, looking around at the others. He was wearing brogues that gleamed in the firelight. A pair of pinstripe trousers peeked out of the bottom of the voluminous robe. I guessed it was a man and he was the leader.

Combat boots slipped their chalk into a pocket, wiped their hands on their robe and nodded at the central figure. The figure wearing brogues raised his hands to the ceiling and the others hastily assembled in a circle around the large drawing on the flagstones. I debated pushing the boxes over and running when I heard an electronic phone alarm sound. The figures in the centre tilted their heads trying to locate the sound. The alarm echoed around the room making it difficult to pinpoint.

Schiztz. It was my phone. The alarm I'd set for sunset had gone off. I reached into my pocket and tried to turn it off. Heads turned in the direction of the boxes. The figure in the centre pushed back his hood revealing an angular face with a waxy shine to it. The torchlight glowed on his bald head and glinted off his neatly trimmed pointed beard. If we were in a different setting, he could have been an oily accountant or a banking clerk. He smiled nastily. It gave him the air of someone about to turn down a loan application.

"It appears our guests have arrived right on time," he gestured with his long hands and four of the hooded figures detached themselves from the circle and walked towards the boxes. I had less than five seconds before they found me.

Clutching Bane, I slammed my body into the boxes. It didn't have quite the effect I'd hoped for. The boxes were empty and I had put too much force into my push. Off balance, I stumbled through the boxes. They scattered on the floor. The figure nearest me raised his hand to deflect the oncoming cardboard onslaught. I crashed into him and he fell to the ground with a grunt, taking the full force of my weight and hitting the stone floor hard. He gave an unmanly high pitched cry as I trod on his fingers. I ground my sturdy boots into his hands. I scrambled to my feet, waving my axe in what I hoped was a menacing way.

Another robed figure approached from the side and grabbed my arm. I spun and managed to club him with the flat of my axe in the stomach. He doubled over, winded. I cried "Sheld" and activated my protection charm to even the odds as more figures approached warily. This close I could see that their robes, which I had taken for black, were actually very dark red. The colour of rich wine or possibly old blood. Somehow that made it more sinister than black.

The man in the centre hadn't moved and was still smiling his clerky smile.

"Where is the elf?"

I eyed the figures surrounding me. One of them made a grab and failed to make contact thanks to my magical barrier. "It's just me."

The man arched a neat black eyebrow and said pleasantly "I don't think so," he made a gesture and a slim robed figure disappeared into the entranceway.

"You're too late! Sunset's passed!" I tried.

The man laughed. It was a clipped laugh, one that didn't come naturally. He shook his head and I saw pointed ears glowing pink in the flame light. Another elf.

"Aha. It doesn't matter. We will succeed!" The red light gave him an ominous glow. Just keep him talking Amethyst. The further it is from sunset, the less likely it is to succeed. The figure returned from the underground passage shaking its head. So they hadn't found Lorandir. I hoped he had a plan.

"So is it a law that crazy cults have to wear robes?" I bantered, "And where do you get them from anyways? Is there a wholesaler for cloaks I don't know about?"

The clipped laugh came again, as if he had read about laughing in the book but had never actually heard it. "Aha. Very good. But enough of this I think!" With a wave of his hand, I felt myself pulled towards him slowly. I gasped, this wasn't meant to happen. My protection charm should stop this.

I saw him frown. This wasn't what he expected to happen either. I had to use that. I made my eyes look wide and frightened, not much of a stretch given the situation. While I held his gaze, I adjusted the grip on my axe.

As I got close to him, I felt his power. It put me on edge. It felt wrong somehow. Elf magic was usually about elements, nature and growth. His magic felt different; twisted. His eyebrows were contorted with confusion while his power dug into me, probing and uncomfortable.

As he reached for me, I swung my axe, fighting against the force pulling me towards him. He saw it in time and grabbed my hand hard. It stopped me straight away.

"How are you resisting me?" he asked the question as if I was a puzzle he would solve. He was talking to himself but I answered.

"Resisting you? Are you trying to spell me?"

It was the wrong move. That raw twisted power coursed around me, through my shield and despite my magic. This elf was truly powerful. I couldn't even cry out. I wanted to curl up against the pain but I was held forcibly upright by his magic. Then he turned it off.

I crumpled to the ground. Bane fell from my hand. The elf smiled nastily again and held out his hand. One of the hooded minions approached, holding out the wooden box subserviently. The elf opened it, and pulled out the Fang Dagger. He held it aloft, looking as if he were in complete ecstasy. A collective sigh of anticipation swirled the room.

Schiztz. He was going to use me as a sacrifice. This was a trap. I tried to squirm weakly away but his magic felt like it had drained me.

At that moment, the figure that had returned from the tunnel walked towards the elf in the middle of the symbol. The elf paused and looked at the newcomer, who threw a blade at his face, then ran the remaining distance.

The elf ducked reflexively but the short dagger grazed his ear as it passed. The newcomer grabbed me and pulled me towards the tunnel. I tried to struggle before I heard a familiar voice. "It's me."

Lorandir! I stopped struggling and allowed myself to be pulled along. The other robed people moved to block our path. We were in trouble.

The bearded elf laughed again, more menacingly this time. "Aha aha. You fools. We don't need your blood to succeed. We will start this ritual now. Tie them up! We'll deal with them later," he added as an afterthought.

We were both grabbed and cable ties were pulled from somewhere under the robes to tie us, hands and feet together. Then the cultists returned to their spots on the symbol.

I watched in horror, as with a faint smile on his face, looking for all the world as if he was solving a particularly difficult crossword, the elf began to speak in Draconic. It didn't sound exactly like the ritual the Professor had read to us.

The chanting paused. The figure closest to the steps approached the centre and offered its hand to the elf. The elf held up the Fang Dagger and drew it across the palm of the cultist. There was a sharp intake of breath then a phrase in Draconic. As the figure withdrew back to its original place, a faint red line of power followed it, linking the figure to the centre.

One by one, each hooded figure approached the centre, had their palm cut and repeated the phrase. After all the cultists had made their blood offering, blood red lines glowed from the elf to the outside of the circle, forming spokes in an occult wheel. Then those on the outer edge joined hands to form a circle. The magic crackled and each of them began to glow a deep red. A magic circle had been created.

The elf in the centre placed the Fang Dagger to his ear and cut it off. He placed the grisly flesh reverently onto the stone floor then continued the chant.

I recognised the phrases now. This was the translation that the Professor and Aloora had done. Schiztz. I squirmed my way towards the circle and shouted out, trying to disrupt the ritual. With a dismissive flick of his wrist, the elf directed a beam of the twisting red magic towards Lorandir and me. It pinned us helplessly to the wall.

The magic beam fizzed up our bodies to our faces. My next cry was choked off as it entered my mouth, reaching down my throat like a fuzzy electric eel. I choked on the hideous texture. It stopped at my vocal chords and stayed there, pulsating, stopping any sound from escaping. I gagged but managed to not throw up. Instead I focused on trying to breathe slowly and shallowly while the magic held me. It was old magic. I had the sense of ancient power mixed with dying trees. The twisted elf magic jarred me. My hands balled into fists on their own.

The elf had finished the ritual now and the symbol on the floor was glowing a dull golden colour. The light rose up off the floor, passing through the red circle and up to the ceiling. It kept going, through the vaulted arches and out of sight. I realised what it was as it floated upwards. A dragon eating its own tail. Poetic.

There were some strange runes floating upwards as well. I guessed they were Draconic, twisting as they went to form strange unwholesome occult shapes.

The chanting stopped so suddenly, the silence filled the room. The bearded elf bent suddenly and drove the Fang Dagger into the ground up to its jewelled hilt. He unfurled slowly, still smiling that clerky smile.

Nothing happened. The hooded figures forming the circle began to look at each other. Combat boots seemed particularly nervous, his hood turning from side to side as he looked at his companions. I started to relax slightly, before choking on the unfamiliar magic lodged in my throat. I was still up a proverbial creek without a paddle but we had succeeded.

A rumbling began deep below the earth. It swelled until the ground was shaking. I felt the wall vibrate behind me, thudding against my body. Then the world exploded.

The floor heaved, and burst apart in a flash of rusty gold light. The leader of the cult jumped backwards, avoiding the chasm that opened under him. Two of the cultists weren't so lucky and fell in. I heard their screams, followed by ominous thuds.

A large scaly head thrust through the hole, emerald eyes blinking as they adjusted to the light. The dragon had awoken.

Its long snout scented the air and it twisted its head from side to side as if releasing a crick in its long neck. It turned, narrowing its massive eyes and let out a roar that made my ears ring. Huge, sharp teeth filled the beast's enormous mouth. It flicked its tongue out into the room, tasting the air menacingly.

Two arms clawed out, thick talons digging into the stone as if it were as unyielding as butter. It heaved its slender powerful body into the room. Large, leathery wings extended upwards as it roared again.

The storeroom we were in was no way near big enough for a dragon. It cracked its head on the ceiling, knocking out several large stones. I tried to squirm against the magical bonds holding me, to no avail. Slabs of ceiling crashed down close to me. The creature growled and bared its teeth. Its pointed tail snaked out and whipped round in anger. It caught a cultist and squashed the robed figure against the cellar wall.

The cultists scattered, pressing back against the walls. Several of them shook their hoods down in the confusion. One stopped next to where I was pinned against the wall and whined "Mama," as he fell to his knees. A thick stench of urine filled my nostrils and I tried not to gag.

The dragon's roar reverberated around the room, deafening me. My instinct was to press my hands over my ears but I couldn't move. Others cowered before it, kneeling and covering their own ears. The dragon noticed them for the first time. It stopped and narrowed its eyes further, emanating power. The torchlight gleamed off of its red flank as it considered the cultists. It snaked its enormous head left and right, the spikes that crested its head glinting ominously.

The bearded elf was the first of the cultists to recover. He stepped forward. He started to say something in Draconic and bowed low in front of the dragon. It bent its majestic head down towards him and opened its mouth. Its flanks swelled with each breath it took.

The others were gazing at it with awe.

The leader smiled up at the dragon. The dragon seemed to smile back, curling its lips up. Its nostrils flared. It made a guttural noise that sounded similar to the Draconic language the elf had uttered. Without blinking an eye, it opened its mouth wider and snapped the elf up. He was gone in two bone-crunching bites.

The red magic threads vanished with the leader. I fell to the floor, my eyes wide with shock. The cultists were screaming now, making for the doorway. The dragon was still hungry. It pulled its large serpent-like body all the way into the room, keeping low to the ground. It clacked its jaws together fiercely as it grabbed the figures with robes.

It was immense. I was awestruck by this creature, frozen as I stared up at it in horror. Larger than the room we were in, every time it turned, pieces of wall and ceiling caved in. We would be crushed. Lorandir kicked me sharply. I turned away from the carnage and saw him gesturing with his head towards the passageway whilst shuffling backwards. I mimicked his shuffle, levering myself backwards on my bottom and pushing with my bound feet. We had nearly made it into the tunnel, when the dragon turned, snaking its head after a cultist. As it manoeuvred in the tight space, its spiked tail whipped round and caught me.

I was flicked across the room, into the boxes. Unable to brace for impact with my hands and feet tied, I was helpless. I bounced off the cardboard and into the wall. I heard something crack and felt pain explode through my side.

I tried to move and the pain intensified. Gasping, I squinted into the room. I blinked to try to focus as two enormous dragons swam in front of my eyes.

Lorandir had made it to the tunnel and pressed himself against the wall. It was better than my predicament, stuck in a room with a hungry dragon. It looked my way, emerald eyes blazing. I stayed still as the creature flicked out its tongue, scenting the air again. I was toast. Possibly literally if it could breathe fire. I hadn't wanted this adventure and now I was going to die.

A movement caught its eye and it snapped its head around. A sulphurous smell filled the room, pungent and sharp. The monster spat out hot white flames, torching three of the Awakeners. I stared in horror as it devoured their charred remains. Its tail whipped round again and connected hard with my head. The world turned black.

Chapter 17

I awoke to the aftermath of chaos. The tangy scent of sulphur hung in the air. Lorandir was leaning over me looking concerned and calling my name while shaking my shoulders. As I blinked away the yellow sparks, his concern turned to relief.

"I thought you were dead," he sounded emotional. I was still waking up and couldn't process anything. He looked dishevelled. Dirt and soot streaked across his face and his long hair had been charred and burnt off. It now fell in jagged clumps, turning from blonde to black towards the ends.

"Don't even worry about it," I panted automatically as I pushed myself upright, sitting heavily against the wall. Pain shot through my side. My thinking was still fuzzy. My hands and feet had been untied. Loose strands of cable ties curled on the stones. The Fang Dagger was resting on the floor, the blade sparkled menacingly in the pale orange light. Light? I squinted. One of the torches had survived the dragon and sputtered weakly in the cellar.

The doorway had disappeared, along with half the steps that led upwards. In its place, a wide opening gaped out, letting in the cold night air. Large stones littered the room, wrested from centuries old walls. The faint glow of city street lights shone weakly through the destruction. Sirens sounded as city life continued outside. Strange dark stains spattered the grey stones.

"Wha..?"

Lorandir filled me in. The dragon had eaten most of the Awakeners, it was not a pretty eater. That explained the stains. I shuddered. A couple of cultists had tried to escape through the doorway. The dragon had chased them, ripping out the heavy door as it exited. Lorandir had crawled on his stomach through the debris to his sword and used it to saw through the bonds tying his hands and feet.

He tucked a filthy matted strand of hair behind my ear and left his hand there. He frowned and then I felt his other hand on my side where a burst of pain exploded along with purple stars in front of my eyes. Then his magic began to course through me.

The combination of honeyed mead and bittersweet chocolate was overwhelming. I moaned slightly.

"Am I hurting you?" his voice was gentle. I shook my head and placed my hand over his, keeping it pressed into my side, the warmth of his magic flooding me. I leaned towards him. It was strangely silent, as if the world had stopped and it was just us, cocooned in this destruction, safe in the midst of disaster. He bent his head over mine, and then we were kissing. It was a deep desperate lingering kiss.

A shout echoed down to us. He pulled away. Was he embarrassed? I frowned. I opened my mouth to ask him why, but then his hands and his magic was gone leaving me feeling empty and alone.

"Over here!" he shouted. I felt inexplicably awful, as if something special had been ruined. A policeman picked his way over to us and spoke into his radio. I stood and brushed off offers of help as we followed him upwards. On a whim, I picked up the Fang Dagger and tucked it next to Bane in my belt before climbing the destroyed steps and blinking in the bright spotlights set up over the entrance. He directed us to a woman in a suit who looked like she was having a bad day.

She introduced herself as Special Agent Jones, and rubbed her forehead. "Do you want to tell me what is the meaning of this?" she sounded pissed off. I thought it was unfair that we were the outlet for her anger, after all, we hadn't done anything except try to stop this from happening.

"Well…A group of crazy cultists managed to raise a dragon and it looks like it escaped and destroyed part of Cardiff Castle." I looked around. Part of the elegant stone wall supporting the main building had fallen, allowing enticing glimpses into the rich interior.

"I can see that," she snapped. She started walking across the mangled lawn inside the castle walls, her heels sinking into the grass, and beckoned for us to follow as she crossed the drawbridge. There were only police cars around, lights flashing blue as they formed road blocks along the main road. A few pedestrians were filming with smartphones while the police tried to push them back.

I heard my name and turned.

Aloora, Marco, Professor Maron and Gunther were all standing behind one of the roadblocks shouting and waving feverishly. I ran over and hugged all of them.

"Do not ever go off with no phone again. We were worried sick," Marco chided.

"Don't worry, I never want to get stuck in a tunnel or underground room with psychos again. Did you do this?" I gestured to the dozen police cars parked across the road lanes.

Aloora nodded proudly. "Yep. We called in a bomb scare here and at Castell Coch when I got your text," Her expression turned serious,

"We wanted to make sure there weren't any innocent people around in case you couldn't stop it."

"Well we didn't, did we? We failed," I was gloomy.

The Professor put his hand on my shoulder in a conciliatory gesture and was about to speak when a clipped voice called out "Elrond!"

Aloora dropped her voice. "And the Professor called up a contact in the Magical Liaison Office, she was pretty pissed but she came along. She's been really interested in what we've found out."

"I think I've met her," I turned to see Special Agent Jones striding towards us.

"Well?" she barked.

I shrugged. A guy in a bomber jacket approached the group and took some pictures, with a proper camera. I smoothed my hair down reflexively, then gave up after my hand got stuck on blue gunk, the lingering reminder of the goliath. Agent Jones glared at him and waved a badge, talking furiously as she drove him away. She rubbed her forehead, somehow avoiding messing up her neat bob haircut.

"Right. Go home, get some rest. We will talk about this later." With that dismissal, she walked away.

Epilogue

I had never been so grateful for the tiny shower in my flat. I stayed in there for over an hour, scrubbing dirt, blood and blue goo off my body with all of my body scrubbers – loofahs, those weird net-like balls, exfoliator, you name it. I went through my entire supply of calming lavender body wash too and washed my hair five times to get out all of the gunk stuck in it. I left the silky conditioner in to try to calm the relentless frizz that my hair was stuck with, knowing that it wouldn't have any significant impact in the morning. I pulled on my well-worn Iron Man pyjamas and sank into bed. Errol curled up on my feet and I slept.

I was woken by a loud rattling at the shop door and Errol growling in guard wyrm mode. Dazed and confused, I pulled on a hoodie and blearily walked downstairs. Agent Jones was there in a smart dark suit, rapping on the window angrily.

I had to go upstairs to find my key and was very tempted to leave her outside, but common sense prevailed and I dug the key out of my slime covered coat and let her in.

"About time."

“Agent Jones, how lovely to see you, please do come in,” my voice was syrupy. She picked up on it and held her hands up in a pacifying gesture.

“Alright, sorry. I need to take your statement and then I’ll leave you be.”

A golden bracelet glinted against her tanned skin, a cat’s head was engraved into it with red jewels for eyes. She caught me staring and tweaked her suit sleeve to cover it again. I realised I hadn’t seen her ID last night, she could be anyone. I asked for it. She pulled it out of her fake patent crocodile skin handbag and handed it over with a roll of her eyes. I made a show of examining it even though I had no idea how to tell if it was real. I handed it back with a half grin.

“Ruth Jones?”

“Don’t even start with any Gavin and Stacey quips,” she warned. I guessed she’d heard them all. “Have you seen the news?”

I shook my head. “I’ve been asleep for… thirteen hours?” I did a double take at the clock hanging behind my counter. It was still working. I never slept for that long. Cultists and dragons really took it out of a girl.

“Was that a question?” Agent Jones raised her eyebrows, was she amused?

“No, no. I just didn’t realise. I need a drink. Tea?”

“Please. Black and one sugar,” I retreated to the forge to make the drinks, leaving her to look around my shop while I woke up properly. The routine of making hot drinks helping to bring me into the world of the living. I brought out the mugs. Without thinking I’d made her drink in the same Little Miss Sunshine cup I’d given Lorandir. Thinking of him brought a pang of guilt that I’d pushed him away when really I’d wanted to pull him closer.

"Are you OK?" Agent Jones studied me carefully. I blushed a fetching shade of beetroot and plonked the mugs onto the counter.

"Right, well let's get started then shall we?" she took out a large notebook and a recording device from her handbag. I couldn't work out how she fitted everything in there and was studying it curiously when she spouted her first question.

"Tell me what happened, from the beginning," she spent the next two hours quizzing me about the events of the past week. She was very well informed and I guessed she'd spoken to the Professor and maybe the others already. I wondered if she had spoken to Lorandir. I'd been so exhausted yesterday, I hadn't even checked where he was spending the night.

Eventually we finished. I'd choked a little when recounting the goliath attack and the dragon exploding out of the floor, but I thought I'd done alright. I was mentally exhausted now and wanted nothing more than to go back to bed.

"Well, your story ties in with what the others are telling me. You were very brave you know that?" Agent Jones' voice had softened, almost with admiration. My puzzlement must have shown on my face because she added quickly, "Stupid but brave."

She packed up her notebook and the recorder into the small handbag and held out a well-manicured hand as if she was expecting something. I stared at her palm stupidly.

"The Dagger?"

"Erm…" How did she know I took it?

"The Magical Liaison Office will be taking that artefact into custody Ms Haernson, would you like me to get a warrant?" Her voice had hardened.

I held up my hands, "No, no, I'll find it," I left her downstairs as I went to find the relic. I hadn't been thinking too hard about the Dagger when I got in last night and after a couple of false starts found it on the floor underneath a pile of soiled clothes.

"I'm glad to see you've taken care of it with the respect it deserves," Agent Jones quipped as I handed it over to her, not bothering to wipe the bloodstains from it. She found a linen handkerchief in her bag and wrapped it around the blade. Then she pushed the Fang Dagger into her handbag and drew out a card. She handed it to me, "I'll be in touch if I need anything else and if you need me, here's my number."

I held the card, debating whether to ask my next question. My curiosity was too high and it wasn't like I was going to see Agent Jones again. I might as well ask. "You don't know what happened to the elf do you?"

Agent Jones considered me but decided not to press for information. I was surprised she had that tact. "He went off with your friends. I spoke to him this morning. He's fine if you're worried."

"I'm not worried," I replied quickly, too quickly. I started to blush again and I pretended to study the neat lettering printed onto the thick card before putting it on the countertop, silently vowing never to get involved with the Magical Liaison Office again.

Agent Jones must have sensed my silent vow as she repeated her offer as she left. "Seriously, call me if you need to."

I locked the door behind her and ran upstairs to check my phone. Out of battery. Schiztz, I had forgotten to charge it last night. I plugged it in then changed my Iron Man pyjama bottoms for some jeans and took Errol for a walk.

It was a fresh day after the rainstorm yesterday. The puddles reflected the blue sky and sunshine brightly. The roadblocks had gone and the city was back to life this morning. I noted that the Cardiff Castle gates were shut with a sign outside. Curiosity got the better of me and I walked over.

It mentioned that Cardiff Castle was regrettably shut for the foreseeable future and was undergoing renovations. That was an understatement. I walked away, following the wall towards the park, glad I couldn't see the destruction inside. I thought I could smell a faint lingering odour of sulphur and smoke though. I imagined the stone animals perched on the wall were laughing at me. I shuddered and sped up.

I felt reinvigorated after trekking around Bute Park. I briefly wondered if the tunnel had led us under the open space before putting it out of my mind. On the way back home, I stopped to buy a paper as I still hadn't caught up on the news.

Blurry pictures of something large swooping upwards out of the castle greeted me. I opened the paper, turning to the main pages and was horrified to see a picture of me looking a mess and Lorandir standing behind me, managing to look handsome even with dirt smeared on his face. Life wasn't fair. I tucked the paper under my arm and ran home. Errol grunted unhappily at the pace and I gave him a large scoop of coal as an apology before making myself another cup of tea and stomping upstairs.

The article was short on facts and long on speculation. They had dug out my name somehow though, and both the Professor and Aloora had given quotes to the press. That would drive her online subscribers up, I thought unkindly. After I'd reread the article, I checked my phone.

Texts from Aloora and Marco asking if I was OK. Missed calls from several unknown numbers, I wondered if that was Agent Jones, glad my phone had run out of battery. My heart flew into my mouth, a missed call from Mum and another from Dad. Schiztz.

I texted Aloora and Marco to let them know I was alive, and surfed the BBC news website for a bit. Articles on the dragon were everywhere along with video clips of something large flying away from the castle. One claimed that the dragon had started to make a nest in the Millennium Stadium. That was not going to be popular with the sports fans. The Wales rugby captain and the Cardiff Blues football team had both commented on that in the sports section I noted. So it had definitely happened and now I was living in a world with dragons. I didn't know any Dwarfish swear words that covered that. I closed the browser.

Then I bit the bullet and called my parents. I deliberately called the landline, I didn't want to risk a video chat.

"Hello?" my Dad answered.

"Hi Dad, it's me."

"Ame! Let me put you on speakerphone, we've been so worried," I heard him pressing buttons and then my Mum's voice came over the phone.

"Hi Ame, how are you?"

"Fine Mum, I'm OK."

"We've seen the news, did you really fight a dragon?"

"No Mum, I was just there when the dragon woke up," that sounded really dumb but she seemed to accept it.

"Thank goodness you weren't hurt. What were you doing there?" Dad sounded curious now he knew I was OK.

"Erm, trying to stop them," that sounded stupider.

"And who was the handsome man darling?" Trust Mum to pick up on that. I rolled my eyes and gritted my teeth.

"Elf, Mum."

"Well he looks lovely, are you seeing him?"

"He's an elf Mum! And no, we were just…together when the dragon came out." That sounded like an innuendo. There was a pause.

"Well we want to see you, we're coming to Cardiff."

I grimaced, I loved my parents but they were always excited by the big city and Mum would force me to go shopping. I still hadn't told her about the red coat. "No, please. I'll come and see you, I need a break."

"You always did work too hard love. Come as soon as you can or we'll come and see you," Dad hung up on that threat.

I groaned. I felt like a teenager instead of a thirty something. How could Mum think I was with an elf? That brought my thoughts back to Lorandir. I needed to pull myself together. It was only a kiss. The best kiss of my life, I admitted to myself. With an elf who I had instinctively disliked when I first met him. And who was gone anyway. We hadn't even managed to stop a dragon being woken up, so it didn't matter. It wasn't like I'd ever see him again.

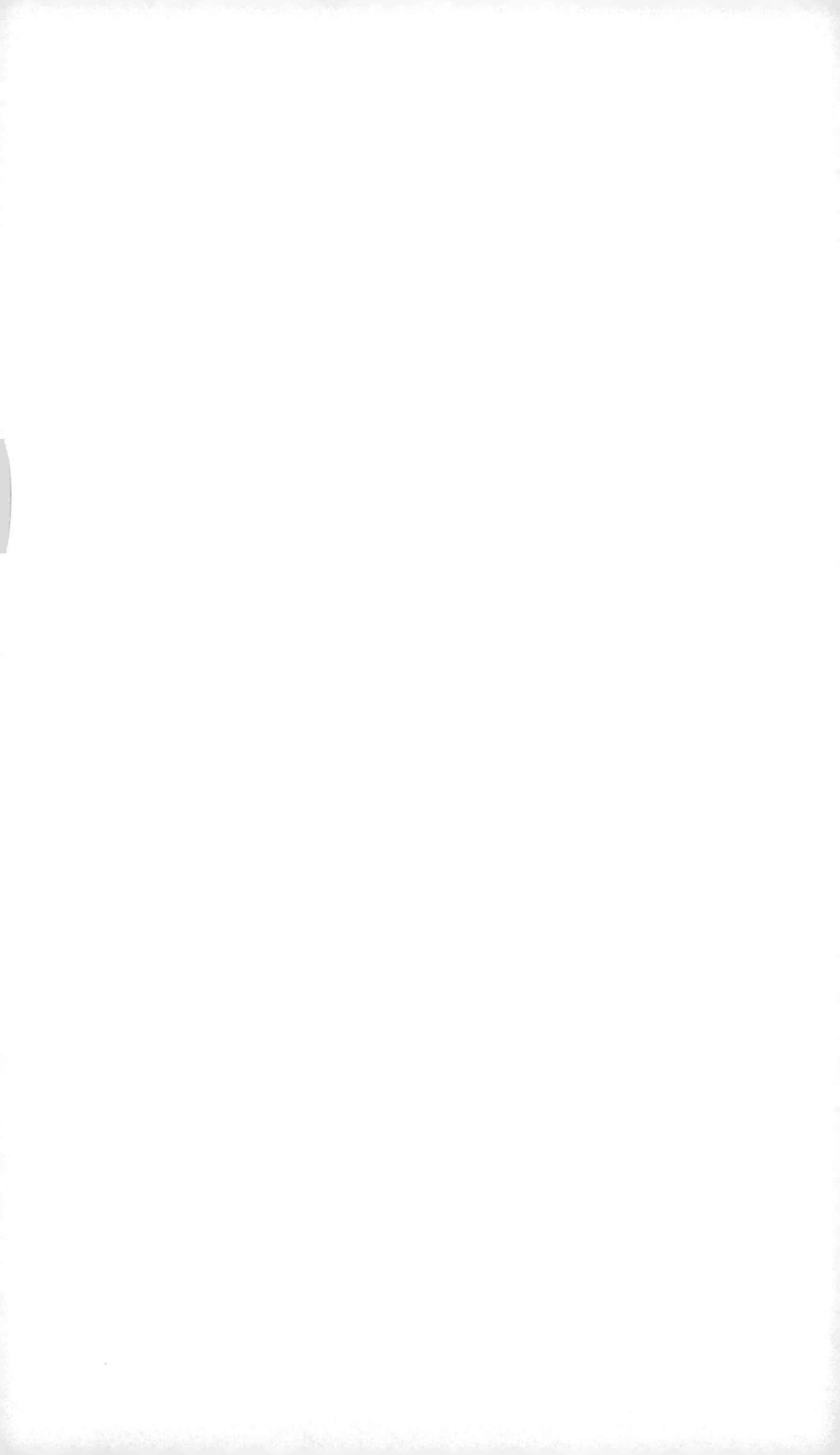

Other Books in This Series

Thank you for reading book one in the Rise of Dragons series. As an independent author, your reviews help me decide which series to keep going so please do leave one on Amazon, Goodreads or any other review site.

If you enjoyed this book, you can get a bonus short story prequel for free by visiting www.gemmaclatworthy.com

You can find book two in the series, Solstice of Dragons, on Amazon or at www.gemmaclatworthy.com

You can also join Gemma on patreon at www.patreon.com/G_Clatworthy or join the readers' Facebook group, Gemma's book wyrms, for updates and chat about dragons. Find Gemma at www.facebook.com/gemmaclatworthy

About the Author

Gemma started writing during the 2020 lockdown and loves fantasy fiction and dragons in particular. She lives in Wiltshire with her family and two cats and also enjoys crafts of all kinds.

She also writes children's books. You can support her on www.patreon.com/G_Clatworthy or you can find out more on her website www.gemmaclatworthy.com or follow her on Instagram (www.instagram.com/gemmaclatworthy) or Facebook (www.facebook.com/gemmaclatworthy)

www.ingramcontent.com/pod-product-compliance
Ingram Content Group UK Ltd.
Pitfield, Milton Keynes, MK11 3LW, UK
UKHW040007200726
13854UKWH00001B/80

9 781915 516015